About the Author

I am a mother of boys, an avid reader, and a lover of literature. I enjoy being creative in any way possible, and believe in living life to the fullest.

Make Believe

Taylor-Jean Paige

Make Believe

Olympia Publishers
London

www.olympiapublishers.com
OLYMPIA PAPERBACK EDITION

Copyright © Taylor-Jean Paige 2023

The right of Taylor-Jean Paige to be identified as author of
this work has been asserted in accordance with sections 77 and 78 of
the Copyright, Designs and Patents Act 1988.

All Rights Reserved

No reproduction, copy or transmission of this publication
may be made without written permission.
No paragraph of this publication may be reproduced,
copied or transmitted save with the written permission of the publisher,
or in accordance with the provisions
of the Copyright Act 1956 (as amended).

Any person who commits any unauthorised act in relation to
this publication may be liable to criminal
prosecution and civil claims for damage.

A CIP catalogue record for this title is
available from the British Library.

ISBN: 978-1-80439-297-3

This is a work of fiction.
Names, characters, places and incidents originate from the writer's
imagination. Any resemblance to actual persons, living or dead, is
purely coincidental.

First Published in 2023

Olympia Publishers
Tallis House
2 Tallis Street
London
EC4Y 0AB

Printed in Great Britain

Dedication

I dedicate this book to my sister, Jessica. You're my cheerleader, my first editor, my number one fan. I love you.

Acknowledgements

Thank you to my wonderful husband for all of his encouragement to pursue my dreams. And thank you to my boys. Without you, I would never have pushed myself to be the best I could be, to be an example worth looking up to. You are my whole world.

PRELUDE

She lay there, trembling from the chill of her own perspiration and the residue left from her horrid dream that somehow felt more real to her than her actual life. But that was absurd, right? How could a dream *feel* real, especially when the dream contained no sense of reality? When the dream was so vile, so horrific, that there was absolutely no possible way it could ever be true.

Yet here she was. Her body ached as if she really had been in a never-ending battle for her life. Her hair was plastered to her head, slick with sweat as if she really had spent the last few hours running until her lungs felt like they were exploding, and her legs had become Jell-O.

She peeled herself off her bed, stretched her strained muscles as she got up. Each movement caused enough pain to send a fresh wave of nausea over her.

Walking slowly, she moved closer to the full mirror that hung on her bedroom wall. She knew what she would see when she reached her mirror. A slender, dark-haired girl, only five foot four on a good day. Hair matted with tangled curls that could never be contained and nearly reached her hips. Caramel brown eyes, probably red rimmed and puffy from waking up so abruptly. Lips that were definitely nothing to brag about; but at least they were always a perfect shade of red and she never needed to wear lipstick, not that she ever really wore makeup except for the daily use of mascara to accentuate her naturally long lashes.

She took a long, deep, nerve-settling breath, and stepped in front of the mirror and almost instantly chuckled out the breath that she thought she had already let out.

All she saw was herself, exactly how she thought she would see herself. Her light blue pajamas with little sunflowers printed on them were ruffled and wrinkled, she had sleep lines on her arms and face. She was just her. Madison, Maddie for short. The same person she had been since she was brought into the world twenty-two years ago by parents that she had never met, in a place that she hadn't been since then and wasn't even sure of the name of.

"It was just a dream, after all," she whispered to herself. And, already, she was forgetting the dream, the way most people do when they wake up and try to think about them. For instance, she could no longer recall exactly how it was she had managed to escape the hand that had clutched so tightly on her throat she saw stars. She no longer had any memory of how she had gotten back home; though she distinctly remembered how that was all she desperately wanted to do as her dream self.

It was just a dream. Even though she knew that was what it was, it was a relief to her to see the remnants of sleep so clearly evident.

She sighed, gave herself a small smile, and turned to go back to bed.

Had she bothered to turn on the lights, or even take another look at herself as she was turning away from her reflection, she may not have missed the half leaf, stuck in her tangled hair, that could not have possibly come from anywhere in her room.

CHAPTER 1

"Wake up!"

I jumped awake and quickly closed my eyes again as the harsh light invaded all of my senses and gave me an instant throbbing headache. My heart was nearly pounding out of my chest, and I struggled to catch my breath.

Squinting, I peered around to check my surroundings. My classroom. I must have fallen asleep during class, again. My philosophy professor was definitely going to fail me. It was the third time this month that I had fallen asleep during his class. In all fairness, it was my most boring class. All we ever did in philosophy was take notes every day, and then end every week with a quiz.

I looked to the perky girl sitting next to me, the source of the wake-up call. My best friend since early middle school.

Ally was standing beside me, her upper body flung halfway onto the table, her face mere inches away from mine. Her breath was warm on my skin and smelled like the sour cream and onion chips she was always snacking on.

"Personal space, please." I smiled and pushed my friend away gently.

"What's going on, Maddie? You up all night with a special someone that you neglected to tell me about?" Ally wiggled her brows and returned the smile.

"As if!" I looked at my best friend, amazed, as always, at how beautiful she was. "We share a room; you would know if I had anyone over."

She was the kind of beautiful that made everyone stop and look. She had the most perfect, straight, brilliantly white teeth I had ever seen. Every time she smiled, she showed off a dimple in each cheek that just made you want to smile. Her hair was the color of honey, and it matched almost perfectly with her eyes, which were huge and always seemed to sparkle. She was definitely blessed in the build of her body too. She had the kind of body most models would kill for.

"Then what's going on?" Ally asked again.

"Nothing, we are going to be late for our next class if we don't get moving." I grabbed my stuff and started making my way towards the door.

Ally and I had been friends for nearly a decade, but these dreams had me so out of sorts, how would I even begin to explain them to her or anyone else? I did not even know how to explain them to myself. 'Ah, yeah, so I have these dreams where I am in a constant battle. And when I have those dreams, for some reason, I wake up extremely sore and exhausted and I feel like I was actually in combat.' Okay, I guess that was a way to explain it, but it is not like that makes a lot of sense or sounds like anything that comes from any type of sane person.

"Actually," Ally said as she caught up to me. "I'm ditching for the rest of the day."

"Why is that?" I asked her, whispering a silent thank you for the change of subject.

"It's my mom's birthday. She told me yesterday that they're flying me back home to spend the weekend with her and her boyfriend. It'll be nice to see Mom, but I am not looking forward to meeting her new boyfriend. I swear, she has a new one every few weeks."

I had been hearing about her mom's endless string of boyfriends for the past few years, ever since her parents got a divorce and her dad moved practically across the globe. Ally did not seem to mind the absence of her dad though. She got to travel the world with him during her summers and spring breaks, and he was paying for her college tuition in full. No student debt for that girl. We are not all so lucky.

"Well," I said, trying my hardest to hide my smile. "This could be your new daddy."

"As if!" she yelled so loud that some of the other students walking across campus stopped and looked our way. "I could never, and would never, call someone 'daddy'. Gross! Anyways, I have to run so I can catch my flight. Don't do anything crazy without me!"

I hardly got another word out before she whisked away leaving me alone and, after a quick confirmation look at my watch, very late for my next class.

Thud.

Before I even knew what had happened, I was on the sidewalk, my philosophy book sprawled next to me, and my notes were slowly fluttering lazily to the ground.

"I am so sorry!" A hand grabbed my arm. "Are you okay?"

"Yeah, I just need to – oh!" The hand that gripped my arm pulled me up so abruptly I was hardly able to register the fact that I was no longer lying on the ground. It took me several seconds to slow down my racing heart and form a coherent thought.

"Here," the stranger said. "Allow me."

I looked to my left and saw a huge man on the ground frantically grabbling all of my papers and books. His back was to me, so all I could really see of him was his massive shoulders, and the way his muscles moved under the shirt he wore. It looked similar to the way water rippled over a pond.

"It's okay, really." I stooped down to help him and he started to stand back up, which resulted in yet another collision. "Ouch!" my hand flew to my nose and the word came out before I fully realized that I had not actually hurt myself. I was such a clumsy person on a normal basis, my mind just automatically assumes I hurt myself every time I get any type of bump.

"I am so sorry!" his voice came.

"I'm fine, really." I looked at him and for the first time saw his face. My heart stopped beating.

I knew him from somewhere, I had no idea how I knew him, or who he was. But I knew him. It was hard to forget a face like his.

The man's eyes were the most electric blue I had ever seen, his face perfectly chiseled, with a square jawline covered in a morning shadow. His lips were full and pink. Right above his perfect lips was the only imperfection on him – his nose had a slight crook to it, obviously from a very old break. He had thick black hair that just brushed the tops of his broad shoulders.

I realized I was staring, but I could not stop. He could not seem to stop either. Neither one of us broke our stare until another student went whizzing by on their bike, hollering for us to move out of their way.

"I'm sorry," I finally managed. It unsettled me so much to see him, and there was absolutely no reason for it.

"No," he said. "I'm sorry. I wasn't looking at where I was going. I'm Ryker."

"Maddie." I dropped to the ground quickly and started to grab my things, completely embarrassed because I realized he did not ask me for my name.

"Maddie," he almost whispered. He got down on my level

and started to help pick up the papers. "Maddie, can I make this up to you, somehow?"

There was no way I was looking at him again.

"It really isn't a big deal. I'm late for class, I really need to get going," I said to the ground.

I jumped up and started to walk away as fast as I could. I knew I had left over half of my notes lying on the ground, but I did not want to be there with him any more. The odd sense of deja-vu was too overwhelming. Besides, Ally took way better notes than me anyways. I would just copy hers. It would not be the first time; I doubted it would be the last.

"Maddie," Ryker called after me. He did not say it in any mean or threatening way at all but, somehow, he managed to say my name in a way that terrified me to my core and made me stop dead in my tracks, sending a chill down my whole body.

"Maddie, come back."

Why did I turn around and start walking back to him? How did he do that to me? It was not necessarily an order; he was speaking softly and calmly. It sounded more like a plea than a demand. Yet, my body blindly followed him.

"Come to lunch with me. You're late for class, anyways. Come with me, and we will talk." Ryker held out his hand.

My mind could not process why my body was obeying his words. Every cell in my brain was screaming at me to stop, walk away, and not look back. Yet my hand reached out to him anyways and my fingers clasped with his. It was the oddest feeling, like I was working on autopilot. I had no control over my movements or mouth. I could not even yell out for help. I was a puppet, and he was controlling the strings.

He led me without another word to a small diner only a few blocks off campus. I had never seen the diner before, but then again, I had rarely been off campus since Ally and I shared a dorm room and ate in the campus dining hall every day, with the rare exception of the local McDonalds a few miles away.

The diner looked run down, the roof seemed like it was already half caved in, and half the windows had some kind of hole or crack in them. There were some window frames with no window left in them at all.

Ryker opened the door that was already hanging off the hinges. It made no sense to me how the building was still open for customers or how the door managed to remain in an upright position.

The inside did not look much better. There were three tables and two booths total. Everything else looked like it had been burned in a fire. Ashes covered the floor; the walls were singed with soot. There were no customers. It did not even smell like a diner. The only thing I could smell was mildew. I looked up and saw that my original assumption about the roof was correct.

There had definitely been a fire here, and since I could smell no remnants of smoke, I could assume that the fire had taken place quite some time ago. There had probably not been a soul in this building in years.

Ryker stopped at a table and motioned for me to sit down.

Run, I commanded my legs. I sat down.

He turned his back to me and I was again fascinated by how muscular his back was. His huge shoulders rose and fell steadily as he took in slow breath after slow breath.

"You recognized me," he said quietly. It was not a question, but I knew he wanted me to answer him.

"No, I don't know who you are." I wanted to cry. Why was I sitting here unable to move, with a strange man who gave me a huge knot in my stomach, in an abandoned diner that had probably not been in business for at least a decade?

He kept his back to me but turned his head around just enough to glare at me from the side.

"Do not lie to me, Maddie. What do you remember?"

I had absolutely no clue what he was talking about, nor did I want to find out. I willed myself with everything I had to get up and run.

Still, I stayed where I was. The only muscles I seemed to have regained control over were those that allowed me to talk. And I was not so sure that I was the one who allowed myself to talk, rather, he relinquished those muscles needed to answer him.

"Please," I whispered. "I don't know what you're talking about. Please let me go." I could not help it, then. Tears flowed down my cheeks and dripped down onto my shirt. I had no control over those either. I was not able to lift my arms to wipe them away.

He whirled around and was an inch away from me before I took my next breath. He had been standing with his back to me at least ten feet away until that moment.

He glared into my eyes; I had no choice but to stare back into his.

"I will ask you one more time," he said so low I could barely hear him despite his closeness. The danger in his voice was pure dominance and threat. "You recognized me; I could see it in your eyes. What, Maddie, do you remember?"

"I don't know." I could not get my voice above an inaudible whisper. "I don't know who you are, please. All I know is you looked familiar. I don't know who you are or why you look familiar. Why are you doing this to me? Why can't I move?"

I really began to cry. My chest tightened and I could not breathe. I knew I was on the verge of a panic attack. I closed my eyes and tried to council my breathing before it escalated to the point where I could not.

Without any warning, my entire body relaxed and almost crumpled in on itself. I opened my eyes and saw that I was completely alone. There were no traces of anyone having been there with me at all. I had not even heard the door open and close, and with the amount of rust on it, I definitely should have.

Nothing was making sense at all. But I knew one thing, I was getting out of there before he showed back up.

I ran as fast as I could and did not stop until I was locked in my dorm room, blankets over me, tears spilling onto my pillow.

It took me several long, agonizing minutes before my breathing evened out and I was able to stop the tears from falling. My eyes burned from rubbing them raw, my body ached from the exerting run, and I had the most massive migraine I had ever had in my entire life. More than that, though, I had no clue what to do about the events that had transpired.

Should I talk to someone? Who would I talk to? What would they say?

Surely, anyone would say I was insane. I would say the same thing if the roles were reversed.

I knew one thing; I would not figure things out by laying in bed crying. I did that; it did not help. I needed to figure out something to take my mind off of everything.

I rolled over and looked out my window. I could not go back out there.

It looked like a normal, sunny day. The students were lazing around the quad. Some were tossing a frisbee, others were sitting down eating their food. Everyone was smiling or laughing. It somehow made me feel even worse.

There was always Ally. I could call her and talk. Not about

the events of the day, she would be the first person to tell me how crazy I was. Knowing her she would probably hound the pilot and force them to turn around, or at the very least cause a huge ruckus trying.

She answered on the first ring.

"Yes, I know we aren't supposed to have our phones on right now, but it's my best friend and she wouldn't be calling if it wasn't an emergency," she said, presumably to the flight attendant that had just reprimanded her for answering her phone on a flight. "What's up?" she said to me.

"I'm sorry, I wasn't thinking. I don't want you to get in trouble, call me when you land?"

"Not a chance," Ally squealed so loud I had to pull the phone away from my ear a few inches. "You are my priority. Besides, I think they just make that stuff up so not everyone is trying to talk over each other on their phones."

"Oh, Ally." Despite the strange and terrifying day, I smiled. I smiled for my best friend. I smiled for her carefree attitude and the way she handled any situation with humor and grace and authority. I bet she would have done everything completely differently than I had.

"So, what's up?" Ally asked.

"I just miss you. The dorm room feels so empty without you. It's kind of creepy, honestly." I scanned the room as I spoke to her. Every corner looked like it could house a new monster. I kept envisioning Ryker popping out from underneath Ally's bed across the room. Everything reflecting in my mirror seemed distorted and ominous. I quickly looked away from the mirror, or at least I tried to. As I stared into the mirror the realization of who Ryker was smacked me harder than any fist ever had.

I dropped my cellphone and stared at myself, feeling my

chest tightening as it became harder to breathe.

"Hello? Hello? Mads, this is not cool," Ally's muffled voice broke my stare and brought me back to the moment. My phone had tumbled to the floor and managed to make its way under my bed.

"Ally," I fumbled with my phone, desperately trying to get it back to my ear. "Ally, I have to go. Call me when you land."

I hung up the phone before she could protest, which I knew she would. Knowing her, she was probably already calling back. She would be pretty upset when I did not answer, but that was not a concern of mine right now.

I climbed out of the comfort of my blankets and inched my way to the mirror without even blinking. I did not want to lose focus, and now that the thought was in my head, I could not believe I didn't think of it earlier. As soon as I saw Ryker, I knew that we had met before, but until now I had no idea how I knew him.

Finally, almost nose to nose with my own reflection, I knew. Ryker was in my dreams. He was there when I was running for my life, when I battled my enemies, and when I felt my life being drained from me as a hand crushed my esophagus.

Ryker was the one I was fighting so hard to get away from. It was his strong hand crippling me, he was chasing me, pushing me to run harder and faster than I ever thought I could.

Why would I dream of someone I had never met before? Is it possible I had seen him walking around campus, or eating in the dining hall just a few tables away? Maybe we had a class or two together and I just never noticed him.

No. I would have remembered him. He was sexy and beautiful. He was the kind of guy I would have noticed right away. And if I did not notice him, Ally certainly would have. She was always noticing guys no matter where she went, and they were always noticing her.

Even if that were the case, and it was just my subconscious bringing this random stranger up in my dreams, why would I be battling him? Would it not stand to reason that if it were my subconscious, I would be seeing him in a romantic way? That aside, it still did not explain the strange things he seemed to be capable of. I had no control over my body around him. And he moved scarily fast.

Maybe today was a dream? Who could say it wasn't? Maybe I was still asleep. Maybe Ally never even woke me up in philosophy class and she did not even leave for the weekend.

That seemed to be the most logical explanation. It was certainly worth a shot. I closed my eyes, held my breath, and counted to ten, willing myself to wake up from this never-ending nightmare.

I would open my eyes and see her sitting next to me, diligently taking notes, with a bag of sour cream and onion potato chips sitting next to her notebook. There would be crumbs everywhere because she was the messiest eater I had ever met, and our professor would be glaring at her as he taught because the bag was noisy, and it distracted pretty much everyone around us.

With the image of her so clearly in my mind, even imagining the smell of her chips and the sound of rustling paper from my classmates, I opened my eyes.

And screamed.

Ryker was standing behind me, glaring at my reflection.

His hand cut off my scream barely a millisecond after I opened my mouth, and then his breath was hot on my neck as he whispered in my ear.

"I'm going to remove my hand, but I am warning you, Maddie. Do not make a sound." Spittle sprayed from his lips as he spoke to me. It took every ounce of my willpower to not wipe it away from my neck and cheek.

His grip loosened slightly from my jaw as if he were testing me to see if I would scream again.

I did not.

Not because I did not want to, but because I was more afraid of what he would do to me if I did.

"Good." Ryker slowly dropped his hand and took a step back.

I could not do anything but look at him in the mirror, standing behind me, chest heaving rapidly as his breath slowly started to even out. I could tell he was trying to keep his own emotions in check.

"Maddie, we need to talk. I'm sorry for disappearing on you, earlier. I didn't want to lose my temper."

I just looked at him. My instant thought was to give him a snarky comment, something along the lines of 'you mean that wasn't losing your temper earlier?' or 'you actually had a handle on that?'. But I knew that would only make things worse for me, so I bit my tongue hard enough I tasted blood, and kept my mouth shut.

"I need you to close your eyes, and do not open them until I tell you to."

"Why do I have to close my eyes?" I protested. I knew I should have just done as he commanded, but the thought of closing my eyes when he was this near was a frightening one.

"Because I told you to. Do not question me."

I closed my eyes.

As crazy as it may seem, the only thought that went through

my head in that moment was how I had the ability to control my eyelids, when earlier he somehow took that ability away from me and controlled them for me.

Since I could not see what he was doing, I tried to use all of my other senses to the best of my ability.

My dorm room smelled like nail polish and vanilla. It was a nauseating aroma to most people, but to me and Ally it smelled like home. We both loved the scent of vanilla. And every weekend we stayed at one or the other's house and gave each other mani-pedis. As soon as we moved into the dorm, we went straight to the store to get an absurdly large amount of vanilla oil for our air diffuser, and when we got back we started working on our hands and feet.

The air was our perfect temperature at seventy-two degrees precisely. We refused to move into a room that did not allow us to control the thermostat. It was perfectly cool enough so that we could comfortably sleep under the mound of blankets that were an absolute necessity, yet warm enough that we could lounge in our tank tops and shorts before, between, and after classes.

The only sounds were of the diffuser puffing out a tuft of fragrant air, and the low hum of my laptop on my desk in sleep mode. I never turned it off, even though Ally relentlessly badgered me about how bad it was on the fans and motherboards and whatever other technical mumbo jumbo she claimed. She can say whatever she would like about me leaving my computer on all the time. That laptop had lasted me for six years and was still going strong. Besides, I liked the noise in the background, especially when she got to go home for the weekends, and I was stuck here because I was not disgustingly loaded like she was.

As these thoughts raced through my head, everything changed in an instant.

I could no longer smell my diffuser, which I knew had just sent out a puff less than five seconds ago. I was no longer comforted by the fumes of the cherry red polish we both used last night.

The temperature dropped drastically, and if I was able to guess I would assume it to be near fifty-five degrees.

Gone was my old computer's soft hum.

Replacing the smells was the awful, overpowering stench of rotting leaves and dirt. That made no sense. We were hundreds of miles away from any wooded area. And it was the beginning of summer. How would there be rotting leaves?

All around me birds were chirping, bushes were rustling, and it sounded like footsteps. They got louder and quicker, matching my rapidly beating heart.

Just when I thought it was going to burst right through my chest and I was going to fall over, lifeless, Ryker spoke.

"Maddie," he whispered. "Open your eyes."

He spoke the words in such a calming way, it sent a wave of instant peace over me, my heart decelerated back into a normal rhythm, and the footsteps had stopped.

For no reason that I could discern, I was no longer afraid.

I opened my eyes, surprised to see how accurate my senses were to picking up on my surroundings.

I was, indeed, in the middle of the woods. Impossibly enough, it appeared to be the middle of fall, by the looks of the leaves smushed into the ground and the bare branches above me.

I spun in a slow circle, taking it all in. How did I go from my comfy home away from home in the start of summer, to the woods that were hundreds of miles away in the middle of fall, all within the span of two or three breaths?

Before I could finish my circle, Ryker was in front of me,

blocking my view of anything else beyond his dominating, huge body.

"Welcome home, Maddie." And then his lips were crushing mine.

CHAPTER 2

"What are you doing?" I pushed him off of me with all of my might and fought the urge to spit the taste of him onto the ground and out of my mouth.

Even though I would never admit it to such a psychopath, he was incredibly attractive. He would be the exact kind of guy I would want to be kissing on any normal day. I could all but hear Ally asking me for every detail and if he kissed as good as he looked.

But this was not a normal day. And he was definitely not a normal guy.

"Who are you?" I demanded. I do not know exactly where my new backbone came from, he still terrified me to pieces, and I wanted nothing to do with him. It seemed to be that being whisked away to who knows where, with a strange guy who I did not believe was human, just to be kissed, broke a dam inside of me and before I could regain control, I was screaming at him.

"No!" I yelled, fists shaking at my sides. "I don't even want to know who you are. I want you to take me home and never, ever, bother me again. I was having a normal day. I was late to class, like I normally am. I was—"

"Are you having your normal dreams, Maddie?" he cut me off.

"What did you say?" I barely even heard my own whispered words after yelling at him so loudly.

"Your dreams, are they normal?"

"What," I spat at him. "Do you know about my dreams?"

He walked over to me and put his hand lightly on my cheek and used his thumb to stroke my cheekbone tenderly. I wanted to back away. I wanted to turn around and run. I wanted to kick him and punch him and scream.

I wanted to go back in time and not look at my watch while rushing to class.

"Maddie," my name on his lips was more of a caress than his hand on my face was.

I was completely immobilized. Not because he was controlling me, but because I had no control over me either. I felt like a deer standing in the middle of the road as an eighteen-wheeler came barreling down on it at seventy-five miles per hour. I could not move. I could only stare at his brilliant eyes that seemed to be trying to read my every thought and emotion.

He kissed me then, the smallest, lightest kiss. It was so light and quick, I almost thought he did not kiss me. The tingle on my lips lasted only long enough to wonder if it had ever actually been there at all.

"I can't explain it. Not because I don't want to, but because there is so much to explain and it's all so complicated."

His eyes turned sad, it gave me the strange urge to reach out to him, to console him.

Instead, I stood there, still paralyzed. If his hand was not on my cheek holding me up, I feared my knees would give out and I would crumple to the ground to rot with the decaying leaves.

"I'm going to kiss you now. The kind of kiss I have been aching to give you since the moment I laid eyes on you." His voice was low and gruff, it sounded like he was under great strain. "I need your permission, Maddie. I won't kiss you unless you give me permission. Please, please say yes."

If he was not standing so close to me, I would not have been able to hear his last few words. He became so quiet in his pleading; I wondered if he had actually said them out loud.

A small part of me wanted to say yes. There was no reason for me to let him, I knew that. And there were so many events from that day that I needed answers to, I could not let him. The little, one-celled fiber in me that wanted him to kiss me was overwhelmed by every other ounce of me. Logic dictated, finally.

I stepped back and away from him. Hurt flashed across his handsome features as he let his hand drop to his side. The hurt was quickly replaced by a mask of cool, collected calm.

"What do you know about my dreams? How do you know about them?" I whispered. I did not trust myself to speak up. It frightened me that he knew about my dreams, the dreams I only remembered him being in so vividly when I looked in my mirror. Standing in front of him, though, the role he played in those dreams was not so clear any more. I could see him in front of me, face contorted in anger, hand clasped firmly around my throat holding me suspended a few inches from the ground. I could also see him breaking the arm of the blurred-out figure holding me, choking the life from my body.

"I know everything about you, about you and your dreams. I never wanted to hurt you. My whole existence has been to protect you, and somewhere along the way I failed. It was my born mission to keep you safe. But I couldn't keep you safe any more. Can't you see that?" He rushed at me again and grabbed one of my hands in both of his, he had tears rapidly pouring over his cheeks.

It looked odd to me, seeing such a handsome, strong man being so vulnerable, allowing himself to cry. Not that I thought that there was anything wrong about a grown man that was in touch with his emotions. It just looked odd to see it. It was like seeing a newborn baby in a karate tournament. It just was not something that most people, normal people, would find typical.

"What are you talking about?" My tears threatened to match his, but I needed to know what was going on. If I let loose and cried, I knew I would not be able to stop long enough to ask the questions I had been dying to ask.

"You were my queen; I was your loyal guard. You are still my queen. You are still my everything; you're the very breath that I take."

"Ryker," I choked on my own voice. My saying his name made him tremble.

We both stood there, staring at each other. I tried desperately to find words to say, anything to either help me make sense of what he was saying, or to get him to take me home so I could finally wake up from this awful nightmare.

Just like in the dreams I had, all I wanted to do was find my way home.

My dreams. I turned away from him and looked back at the woods surrounding me. This was where I ended up in every dream, this exact spot. Once I reached this spot I could wake up.

I needed to know for sure, but I somehow knew this area. It dawned on me that I knew exactly where I was. Testing my theory, I walked to a dying tree about ten feet away from me. It was massive, easily one of the oldest trees in the immediate vicinity. There was no way I should be able to know that, I knew nothing about trees other than the fact that they were made of wood and housed birds and other critters. But I realized I did not *know* it was old, I *felt* it was old.

If my thoughts were correct, there was a carving on the other side of this tree. It would be just two simple letters: MR.

In my dreams, I assumed it was someone who had started to write their name, or maybe sketched in their initials and planned on finishing it when they found their special someone.

Now, though, it was either going to confirm or deny my own craziness. If the letters were there, I was definitely insane. If not, then I was still a loon, but maybe there was hope for me.

I took a steadying breath and worked my way to the other side of the tree's massive trunk, committing each detail to memory as I went.

At exactly eye level, staring right back at me, were the slanted letters.

Yet again, I was unable to move. I was not even able to form a thought, as if my brain stood frozen in time too.

Distantly, I became aware of someone behind me. I knew without turning around that it was Ryker.

"I need to know what's going on." The tears I was fighting so hard to hold back started to silently rain down my cheeks and over my chin.

"I wish I had the words to tell you." Ryker stepped closer to me, close enough that the immense heat radiating from his chest warmed my chilled back.

I leaned back into him. Not because I trusted him, but because I did not trust myself. I felt alone, scared and lost. He was warm, and I needed something solid to help hold me up because if I did not have support, I knew I would fall. I feared if I fell, I would never find the strength to get back up.

He put his arms around me, and I could feel his contentedness as he nuzzled into my hair.

"You know, I have held you like this a million times, and even if I could hold you for a million more, I would never tire of feeling you in my arms."

"Can you answer something?"

"I can't explain it all to you. It would take far too long, and I don't think you can handle it all in the state you're in."

"That's fair." I ceded to his point. I was in such a bad emotional state, I wondered if my body could just simply stop and, if it could, would it? But there was one thing I really wanted to know. "If you had feelings for me, why is it you controlled me earlier, and vanished into thin air? Why did you get so angry with me?"

His whole body stiffened. I sensed that I had struck a nerve with him, though I had no clue what it was. There was a lot lately, I realized, that I had no clue about.

"That is hard to answer. I want to share with you everything. I want to be open with you. I can say, I wasn't angry with you. I was angry at myself. I know you can't remember what we shared; I know I needed to keep my distance. I didn't. I was careless."

"Why can't I remember?" I whirled around to face him. The most infuriating part of all of this was that I was not surprised at all by anything he was telling me. I did not believe it, but I also was not surprised by it, which really only further added to the confusion.

"I can't explain that, either. Maddie, you have to believe me when I say that I would never hurt you, and I would explain it all to you if I could."

"Can you just please take me back to my dorm? I'm tired, I'm overwhelmed and scared." I sighed. I had no idea what to do or say, other than to beg to go home so I could go back to my comfy space in my bed and never, ever leave it again.

"Close your eyes, my Queen," he whispered as he wrapped his arms around me and hugged me close.

I did as he asked for the simple fact that I wanted to get in my own bed and try to pretend this day had never happened. Nothing was making sense. It did not seem like I had anything stable in my life any more.

I had no idea who this man was, what he was talking about, or what I could do with any of the events of the day.

"Open your eyes, darling." He was no longer holding me, and I collapsed.

Luckily, he must have figured I was going to faint, because my last coherent thought was that I was grateful I fell back into my bed, and not onto the tough, carpeted floor.

I had woken up, but I was not ready to face anything or anyone. I laid where I was, unmoving, refusing to open my eyes and acknowledge the new day. The morning sun that slanted through the window blinds was warm on my face. I was perfectly cocooned in my plethora of blankets. It was one of those extremely rare moments when not a single inch of me was uncomfortable.

So, I lay there with my eyes closed, feeling the peace and serenity that comes along with the total comfort that only comes along once in a blue moon.

I knew it was early morning by the way the sun was hitting me. From spending the last several months in that dorm room, I knew when and how the sun shone through the window slats. It felt glorious, like the sun was not only warming my skin, but it was also lovingly embracing my tired soul.

Bliss was the only word I could think of to describe the feeling I had.

Then it was gone.

The blissful feeling, the serene comfort, the warm sun. All of it was gone, in a split moment.

Even with my eyes still closed, I could see the light darkened to black, and my exposed face became chilled.

I knew Ryker was there, standing before me, before I even opened my eyes.

"Go away." I was not ready to get up. Until he took away my warmth and comfort, I believed, even for just those few moments, that everything yesterday had been another long, horrible dream.

I felt his presence in the room before he stepped in front of my window. I chose to ignore it, wanting to desperately believe that it was just leftover remnants of the awful dream I was trying to pretend yesterday was.

"Maddie," my name was a whisper on his lips, and it made me shiver more than the lack of sun did. His voice was so incredibly sad. Even though I wanted him gone, I could not stand to hear that kind of sorrow in anyone and not try to comfort them. I had always been a nurturing person, for as long as I could remember.

I opened my eyes and sat upright so that I could look at him in an attempt to see what ailed him so intensely that it would cause him to sound that miserable.

He was beautiful. The sun framed him from behind and made his already flawless features look like they were glowing. It gave more definition to his massive, muscular profile and enunciated his square jaw.

I was right in my assumption, he looked positively heartbroken.

"Ryker…" I had no clue what to say. I did not know him; I had no idea how to console him. All I could think of doing to help was reaching out to him and taking him by the hand.

His head had dropped so that his chin was resting on his

chest, and the shaking of his shoulders told me he was silently crying.

I took his hand in mine and laced my fingers with his.

His whipped his head back up and he looked at me so intensely, the anguish in his eyes so apparent, my heart stopped beating and I cried too.

I cried for him, and whatever it was that caused his heart so much pain. I cried for what was becoming of my life; I still had no clue what that even was. I cried for all of the unknowns and mysteries that I had been presented with. And I cried a lot because I did not have my very best friend in the whole world beside me to help me work through everything.

"Maddie.," My name caught in his throat. He glanced down at our clasped hands and then looked back to me. "My love, please don't cry."

Ryker pulled me into his arms and held me.

My attempt to comfort him ended up in his comforting me. It was weird how that worked.

I peeled my soaking wet face off of his chest and reached up to touch his face, much like he had touched mine yesterday. He melted into my hand and his whole body shuddered like just the touch of my hand to his cheek was pure pleasure.

At that moment, I could not help myself. I stood up on my tiptoes because he was so much taller than me, and kissed him lightly. I did not think I was capable of such a tender kiss, especially since the only boys I had ever kissed were in high school and college, and they were all, well, high school and college boys. I never had a sweet, innocent, tender and caring kiss.

Until then.

I did not kiss him because I was interested in him, or in

pursuing anything with him. I kissed him because he was sad, and he needed comfort. I kissed him because I had a heart that was too big, and I cared far too much about people, even people who probably did not deserve so much love and care.

As my lips brushed against his, Ryker slowly wrapped his arms back around me, closing me to him tighter and tighter until I could feel his strong heart thundering under his massive chest against my much smaller one.

He smelled like cherries and vanilla. Normally I would question why a man smelled so feminine, especially a man that exuded such masculinity. It just seemed to fit him, though.

His kiss tasted like mint.

His arms felt like home.

He deepened the kiss slightly, as if he was asking my permission.

I allowed him.

As he explored my mouth and I explored his, desire flooded me.

It must have poured into him, too, because his hand moved from the small of my back and found its way to the back of my head and fisted in my hair.

I was distantly aware of the fact that I was moving backwards. I was fully aware whenever I was pinned between the wall and his body, which was equally as hard as the wall but much more inviting.

The kiss deepened further and became more intense, and I no longer cared that I was pinned against the wall. I no longer cared about his one hand fisted tightly in my hair, holding my head steady as he kissed me while his other hand rubbed up and down the front of my thigh.

The kiss was intoxicating. For the first time in my entire life,

I could feel the fire that everyone talked about feeling if you were ever lucky enough to find your soul mate.

How could this stranger be my soul mate? All I knew about him was that he could move incredibly fast, he had the annoying habit of showing up at the oddest and most random times, and he spoke complete gibberish about a life that we were supposed to have together and the love we supposedly shared.

I could not deny how his lips on mine made my chest tighten with anticipation and lust. I also could not deny how everywhere his hands touched left my skin tingling. Or how the scent and taste of him made every cell in my body buzz with excitement, more alive than I ever felt.

But he was still a stranger, and despite how amazing the kiss was making me feel, I knew I should not be kissing him.

Achingly soon, I broke the kiss and bowed my head so that he could not assault my mouth again, and so that I could get a breath in to clear my head from the twisting and dizzyingly terrifying thoughts about how I wanted to kiss him again.

I was completely muddled and confused. I knew I did not really want to kiss him, but I could not deny how life-changing that kiss felt, or the way it made my insides feel like jelly.

"Maddie," Ryker said with a strained whisper. "Maddie, will you come with me? I want to show you something."

I picked up my head just enough to peer at him through my lashes, afraid that if I looked at him any more directly than that, I would end up lip-locked with him again.

"I know what you're thinking." He smiled for the first time since I met him, really smiled. It lit up his whole face and somehow made him impossibly more beautiful than he already was. "I always know what you're thinking. I won't take you away for long. I just want to show you something, hopefully it will help you remember."

Ryker laced his fingers through mine, raised my hand to his lips and lightly feathered kisses along my thumb and onto my palm. I felt the electricity of those few kisses throughout my whole body.

I wanted, more than anything, to go back to my bed. My body ached from the extreme excitement, my mind was tired, my heart was sad. But the thought of possibly making sense of what was going on was too irresistible.

I did not trust myself to speak yet, so I nodded and closed my eyes, anticipating him asking me to close them anyways.

He kissed each of my eyelids with velvety soft lips,

Open your eyes, my Queen. I felt more than heard him say.

How could I feel someone say something?

I opened my eyes, expecting to be in those woods again.

I was not.

Instead, he had taken me to a magnificent bed chamber that looked like it came right out of a castle.

The bed itself was the size of at least four normal king beds, with a massive canopy of the finest silk hanging above it. The blankets were a deep red wine color and matched the canopy perfectly. The bed housed at least two dozen pillows that looked fluffy and light and reminded me of a cloud.

The beautiful, giant bed was in an even more massive and elaborately designed room. I estimated the room itself to be the size of at least two football fields. It had the lushest, most inviting black carpet, and my bare feet were almost completely devoured by it.

The ceiling floated a surprising distance above me, at least three stories high. Even with it so far away, I could see every immaculate detail, clearly hand painted, of a young man and woman embracing each other, painted over and over again. The young couple were painted at least three dozen times, every pose was different.

I the middle of the domed ceiling hung a brilliant chandelier that seemed to be translucent yet rainbow all at the same time. It did not have a single lightbulb on it, yet cast off enough light to keep the entire room brightly lit.

As I looked further, I realized that the chandelier was made entirely of crystals, and it was reflecting the sun from the two walls that were made entirely of window. Without even going to look out, I could tell that I was very high up. There were clouds on the other side of the marvelous, impeccably cleaned glass.

"Where are we?" I asked.

"Does this room remind you of anything?" he replied.

"No." As much as I wanted to have some profound feeling or memory, the room, though absolutely stunning in its beauty, did not remind me of anything or look familiar at all.

"I wasn't sure if it would or not, it was worth a try." He looked around the room, as if he were taking in all the details one last time and wanted to commit them to his own memory.

"What is this place?"

"It used to be your chambers, long ago." His gaze fixed on the bed.

"Did you ever join me, there?" I gestured towards the massive bed.

I knew what his answer was going to be, and even though I was still convinced I was in a long dream I could not wake up from, I wanted to ask him.

"No."

That was not the answer I was expecting. I had thought he would say we had.

"Not that I didn't want to," Ryker quickly added and then chuckled softly. His cheeks blushed and I knew he was nervous. "I mean, of course I wanted to. But you were – are my queen. I could never, unless I was invited. I was never invited."

"Say I was your queen, and we were in love, as you claimed. Why wouldn't I have invited you to stay with me?" I was baffled.

"I don't know if I can explain it. I'm not sure if it will even make sense to you if you don't remember anything." He shrugged. It was the most normal shrug in one of the most unnormal situations I could have imagined.

I laughed, hard. I laughed so hard my eyes watered and my ribs hurt. It took me a solid five minutes to get myself under control. I had no reason to laugh so hard, but his casual shrug seemed so out of place, like if you walked into a movie theater and saw a buffalo sitting in one of the seats eating popcorn and drinking soda from a straw. It just made no sense. I had become hysterical, and it was a struggle to regain control.

"Are you okay?" He was trying to hide his own smile. Surely my absurd outburst had the same effect on him that his shrug had on me.

"Yes, I'm sorry. I just don't know how to deal with all of this. Let's try this again." I took a steadying breath. "Can you try to explain it to me? Seriously, nothing here is making any sense, anyways. At least humor me and try to explain something."

He stared at me for a minute, I could practically see his thoughts flashing across his eyes. He was debating if I was ready to hear anything, and then if I would believe it if he did tell me. Lastly, he wrestled on deciding if it would do me good or more harm. I could see when he finally landed on the decision to try to explain it.

"Okay," he said slowly, keeping his eyes locked on mine.

"You never invited me to your bed because we have a forbidden love. I am your born protector; we cannot have relations. You have invited many men into you bed, but none of them have been me."

"I have had many men?" I was genuinely shocked at that. In all my life, I was never able to go through with sex. I had had a couple of boyfriends, and of those only two were serious. And whereas I loved a good make out session, I would always freeze up when anything would get too heated up or too physical. Even if I thought that I wanted it, and wanted it with that particular guy, even if I had spent the entire day daydreaming to Ally about how that night would be *the night*, it never seemed right. The fact that Ryker was standing here in front of me telling me I had invited many men into my bed was absolutely ludicrous.

"I know that seems insane, but if you could only remember who you are, what your station is, then it wouldn't seem so strange to you. The whole kingdom only wants to please you, it doesn't matter how. Some make the most amazing foods for your table, some heal any ailment that might become of you, and then there are those that are pleasing to you in your private chambers." Ryker shrugged and looked away from me towards the window. "We need you to come back to us, even though it would be dangerous for you."

I entertained the notion that there was a whole kingdom at my fingertips that would stop at nothing to make me happy. What a thought! If only it were real, that would be a pretty amazing concept.

Was it possible that this kingdom he talked about was actually real, and maybe I could see it from the window? We were incredibly high up; I was sure I could see miles and miles of the land below me. The only thing that stopped me from marching over to the wall made of window was the unforgettable and horrifyingly present fact that I was terrified of heights. Even walking along the skybridge from one end of campus to the other gave me goosebumps, and the skybridge was only a second storey bridge. Every time I was any higher than being planted directly on solid ground, my hands got sweaty and clammy, my heart would race, and I thought I was going to faint.

"You don't need to look, not yet. I just wanted you to see your chambers. I hoped it would at least look familiar to you. It's okay that it doesn't." Ryker laced his hands through mine again and began to steer me away from the beautiful bed and the dreadful windows.

"It's okay, I want to," I lied. The truth was, no real part of me wanted to walk to that window. I wanted to completely ignore it, look right past it and pretend it was just a fantastically painted wall. But something urged me deep within to take the chance. Maybe it was because part of me was still clinging to the slight hope that this whole last day and a half had been an awful, way too realistic dream. I still had a chance of waking up and being able to laugh at myself for coming up with such a crazy and creative nightmare.

"I'm here with you, forever and always, my Queen." He squeezed his fingers on mine as if to remind me that he was still holding my hand and would walk there with me and gave me a boyish half smile that made me instantly smile back.

I walked to the window as fast as I could so I would not lose my momentary, albeit fake, confidence. I had the overwhelming feeling in my stomach that if I could face this window, I would wake up. Or at the very least, I would be able to confirm my theory of this all being a dream.

I turned my brisk walk into a full-on sprint, which was

truthfully not very fast since I was not the athletic type at all. I was certain that Ryker had absolutely no problem keeping up with me and was probably slowing himself down quite a bit to boost my own ego. I could appreciate that. He was lending me the confidence to go forward, and even though I saw through the tactic, I respected him for it. It's like when a mother lets her five-year-old win at a board game. It is not so the child does not lose, but rather to build up their confidence in themselves.

Ryker was trying to build up my confidence. It helped.

I stopped a few paces from the window, held my eyes shut and took a few steadying breaths. I could not imagine simply going up to a view that high when I was already out of breath from my clumsy run across the chamber floors. I definitely needed to steady my breathing before I took on the new challenge of looking at the ground miles below.

"Are you sure about this?" his voice was a soft caress in my ear, it sent chills down my spine.

It was now or never. It was time to wake up.

I was ready.

Ryker squeezed my hand once more, and I took the few steps forward, closing the distance between me and whatever fate lay on the other side of that glass.

The scene before me was incredible.

I was obviously very, very high up off the ground, yet I could see everything below me so clearly, as if someone had rigged a gigantic, powerful magnifying glass to the window so that all of the people that should look like ants looked more like Barbie dolls. I could see kids playing in the streets, and mothers and fathers cooking dinners on their grills or mowing their lawns. It looked like such a regular scene; it did not make sense to me that Ryker could think I would not be ready to face it.

"What do you see?" Ryker asked me. His voice was sad, which made no sense to me, either. There was nothing bad about the village below. It looked quiet and happy, friendly, even. "What do you see, Maddie?" he asked again, impatiently.

I told him what I saw. I told him about the three kids playing soccer in the middle of a back alley, of the mother sitting in her swimming pool holding her toddler, letting him splash all around. I told him of the beautiful flowers blooming on the dogwood trees, and the apples that were being picked by a woman with a giant wicker basket. I vocalized to him every magnificent detail that I saw, leaving nothing out.

He was quiet when I finished, staring out the window at the village below.

"You still don't believe any of this, do you?" his response was not accusatory or mean. He sounded like a boy who had lost all hope.

"Believe what, Ryker?" I gestured toward the room and window. "That I am a queen to some race I don't even know the name of, that those are my subjects who are willing to do just about anything to make me happy, including spending private time with me in this ridiculous room, and I am not able to remember any of it, yet you aren't able to tell me why. How am I supposed to believe any of that?"

He grabbed my hand quickly and viciously and crammed my palm against his chest. His heart was hammering into my palm.

"Believe this, Maddie. Believe in me, that I'm trying so hard to do what's best for you, for your kingdom. Believe that I would go to the ends of the earth to do what you asked me to. Believe that the heart you're feeling right now is real, and that it belongs to you even if you can never remember again." He slowed down and took a breath before continuing. "Believe in the love we have, Maddie. The love that you can't deny you felt in that beautiful kiss we shared. I felt you spark to life again, just for a second. I felt you, Maddie, and I need you to believe that."

I wanted to believe him. I wanted to be able to imagine that this craziness was actually not that crazy, and that things like this could be possible. I wanted to believe that I was somebody important, whoever or whatever that may be. And, most of all, I wanted to believe that the kind of love he was talking about was real, and that I was capable of feeling it about someone and them feeling it for me in return. I just could not. It was too much.

And there were far too many things that just made no sense, things that were left unanswered. Things that he left unanswered.

"What are you? And don't tell me you're my lover, or my protector or anything. What are you, Ryker?"

He gave me the same calculating look he had given me before he told me what the room we were standing in was. I knew he was trying to figure out if he should tell me or not. I could see his internal struggle, the battle he was waging within himself, and I knew that, no matter what, if there was nothing else I could believe from him, I could rest assured knowing that he would never do wrong by me. At least, not intentionally.

I trusted him, oddly enough. Seeing him weigh every word with such care and careful calculation helped in ways I had no clue I needed.

Now I needed him to trust me in return. I needed him to trust that I wanted to believe. So far, I had not been scared off. Chances were, at that point, not much more could make me want to run.

"Please, Ryker." One of my hands was still being firmly held in place against his heart, so I took his other hand in my free one and placed it to my heart. "I just need one thing to make sense. I need one thing answered. I need some way to explain why my heart is beating in the exact same rhythm as yours."

"Your heart doesn't beat with mine, Maddie. It is my heart that beats with yours. My whole existence was made to love and protect you. I was crafted specifically for you."

"That doesn't make any sense to me." I closed my eyes, trying to find the words I could use to help me explain how it was I was feeling.

"I know. I want to tell you everything. I want you to be with me and feel for me the way you once felt. I want you to know, to remember."

"Then help me!" I closed the distance between us, crushing our arms and hands as they remained crisscrossed between us, feeling our synchronized heartbeats.

He closed his eyes, it looked like he was memorizing the feel of us being so close.

"Please." I laid my forehead on his chest and closed my eyes. I felt like just giving up and asking to go home and for him to never seek me out again. I wanted to go back in time and ask Ally if I could join her in going home for the weekend. Her parents were loaded, it would have been no trouble at all to get a plane ticket and leave campus. If I had been smart enough to do that, none of this would have happened to me.

"The closest thing to describe us, is human. I know that isn't what you want to hear, and it doesn't help much, but that's the most accurate way. We are most like the humans you are used to. We require the same sustenance as humans. We need food, water, and sleep. We need to exercise and relieve ourselves, the same as humans. The only difference, really, is that some of our abilities are amplified. We can move at incredible speeds, we can live much, much longer, though we aren't immortal. We have very limited powers of coercion and can influence the emotions of others to varying degrees. Not all of us have all of these abilities, and some of us have better control over it than others. For instance, I excel in every ability. I have to, in order to be your protector. Those people down there, they aren't quite as adequate with most of their abilities, and they usually only have one or two supreme capabilities. But we are all special. Some believe we are simply just a race of mutated humans."

"And what do you believe?" It did not pass over me that he had said some believe, and not that he believed.

He studied me again, it somehow reassured me.

"I believe we are unique." Ryker started slowly and carefully.

He knew perfectly well that did not answer my question. He should also know that I would not settle for that. In case he did not figure that out, I gave him a blank stare and held his gaze until I could see that he would continue telling me exactly what he should have said the first time.

"Okay," he continued reluctantly. "Even though I don't think you're ready to hear any of this, I know how to pick my battles."

Ryker pulled away, keeping our hands clasped together and walked me towards the center of the room, away from the windows. He sat me down in a chair that I did not remember seeing in the middle of the floor, and he sat down in a matching one facing it.

Ryker let go of one of my hands, squeezed my fingers in the other, and took a long, low breath, his minty smell invaded my nose.

"We are not human. We only have the capability of mimicking them, in appearance and actions. We do actually have the same basic needs as a human, as I said. But that is where the resemblance ends." He shook his head, clearly not wanting to say anything more, but relenting because I asked it of him, and he served me. "We are fairies. I know your mind instantly went to Tinkerbell."

It did, indeed, go straight to Tinkerbell. The people I saw down below showed absolutely no resemblance to Tinkerbell, or any other fairy I had seen on TV. He laughed, presumably at the dumbfounded look I had plastered on my face. I could not see myself, but by the way my face muscles were contorting I can reasonably assume I would probably be laughing at me if I could see myself too. I relaxed my features and tried to look at him with, what I hoped was, a look of passive interest.

"Go on," I urged.

He smiled that boyish grin at me but continued regardless.

"Maddie, we aren't pixie fairies. They are nasty little buggers. We are a much more... evolved race of fairies. We hold a certain order to the world."

"Okay." I turned that thought over in my spinning head and figured I could allow myself to amuse the notion. "If we aren't pixie fairies, which are nasty, then what exactly are we?"

"Ah, that is the question. You, my Queen, haven't named us yet."

I was completely shocked. I was supposed to name this race of evolved fairies? Why had I not named them yet?

"Here is a very, very shortened version of our history. We used to be an enslaved race. You helped lead us to freedom." He shrugged both shoulders like it was no big deal, like he might have been telling me the pizza he had for dinner last night had anchovies on it.

"And how did I do that?" I knew I was almost shouting, but I could not help it. Everything he told me only left me with more questions, and by that point I was getting fed up with all of the unknowns multiplying before me.

"That's irrelevant to the story. The point is, you did. Since we were such a low caste of fairy, we had no real name. We were only bred from upper castes to do their dirty work, whatever it was at the time. We rose in power and station quickly, under your rule. We waited patiently until you found a perfect name for us. With fairies, names become power. Though we are already a powerful race, once we are properly named our power will multiply exponentially."

"Then why didn't I name you?"

"Well." His eyes narrowed, and he seemed to look past me instead of directly at me. "We had too much work to do. There was battle after battle, war after war, threat after threat."

"I don't get it." There was a major hole in what he was telling me. "If names bring power, why wouldn't I have made something up to give us more power to fight off the threats?"

Ryker's electric eyes lit up, his face brightened, and he visibly relaxed in his seat.

"That is a really good question. You see, the right name brings the right power. The stronger, and more accurate a name is, the more powerful we would be as a whole. You were taking your time, doing everything you could to find the right name for us. If you named us something that wasn't right, we could risk all of our progress and power being stripped away."

That made sense, kind of. Not really.

"Why can't I remember any of this?" I asked for what seemed like the hundredth time in the last day.

"In order to save you, we had to wipe your memory."

"Save me from what?"

"I can't answer that."

I glared at him, and he levelled my look with his own.

"As your queen, I demand to know everything." It was worth a try. If his whole existence was to serve me, it only stood to reason that if I commanded it, it would be so.

"Nice try." He laughed and quickly sucked in his breath. "It didn't work." His words were barely audible, and he looked pained and shocked, as if I had physically struck him. Not that it would hurt him much if I did. I was so small, and he was so incredibly large.

His bright eyes, that just moments ago sparkled, dimmed noticeably and crinkled halfway closed. The beautifully sculpted lips that I knew from experience tasted like life hung slightly apart from each other, and his body had slumped back into his seat. The shocking thing, though, he dropped my hands completely. I had forgotten that he was even still holding them, it felt so normal to have my fingers intertwined with his. Now that he was no longer holding them, they felt cold and lifeless.

I did not understand what had changed him so much, not when he was actually talking to me and giving me the information I so desperately wanted.

"What?" I searched his handsome face for any clue as to why he had changed so much, or why what I said affected him the way it did.

"It didn't work," he said again, tonelessly.

Ryker was no longer looking at me at all. His eyes were vacant and staring past me. He closed his mouth, but it no longer looked boyish and sexy, it no longer showcased a perfect row of dazzling white teeth.

"Why is that such a bad thing?" I never wanted to see this beautiful man looking so sad and beside himself ever again. I could not understand why, but I wanted to do everything I could to bring life back into his features, to see him glow again and see the sparkle that never left his eyes.

"You're my queen. I was made to serve you. If your command doesn't work on me, you're no longer my queen."

That stung on a level I did not think possible. Even if I did not believe in the stories he was telling me, the thought of being someone so amazing, so adventurous as a fairy queen that led her race to safety was incredibly exhilarating. I did not want to lose that feeling of importance and responsibility. But mostly, for whatever reason, I did not want to lose Ryker.

That was ridiculous, right? I had known him for a full day, and already I was dreading losing him. He had done nothing but cause emotional turmoil and more confusion than I had ever thought possible, but he had become very important to me.

I could speculate that it was because, in this dream, he was not only the person that started all of this madness, he was also the person who was helping me to figure it all out, and was the only constant I could think of.

"I want to believe," I whispered before my mind had the chance to fully catch up to my mouth.

His head snapped up, and there was a dull flicker in his eyes that told me there was still at least an ember of hope left in him. That was enough for me.

"Really?" He sounded skeptical. It was odd to me that after all of this, he would be the skeptical one.

I mean, I was living a normal, college life, and he just showed up spewing all of this nonsense about me being some ridiculously awesome fairy queen. Yet he was the skeptical one just because I said I wanted to believe?

"Yes," I admitted. "I want to believe that I am important, and that I am dependable and strong and powerful. I want to believe that I am loved and respected. What woman doesn't want to believe in that?"

"Oh, my love, you are all of that and so much more. Even if you never remember, never lead our race again, if you're never able to tap into those beautiful powers of yours, you'll always be so much more than that." He was off his chair and kneeling down in front of me, burying his huge head into my stomach, enclosing me once again in his hard arms.

I must admit, it felt really good to be so adored, if even by one person who may or may not be a figment of my imagination.

The urge to run my fingers through his hair was beyond tempting. I stared at the back of his head for the first time. I took in the slight curl in his hair, the odd color. The color reminded me of something, though I could not place where I had seen it before. It was a deep, dark black. In the lighting of the massive windows, amplified by the dazzling chandelier hanging directly above us, his dark hair shimmered with a purplish hue. It was very subtle, but it was there. I liked that color.

He relaxed into my lap, and I realized I was no longer refraining from touching his hair.

My fingers twirled along his curls, the purple shimmer rose and fell across the strands as the light danced off his locks.

The texture was like nothing I had ever felt before. I took very good care of my hair, you had to when your hair was a massive ball of curls that matted every time you moved an inch.

Even with all of the hair care products I used on a daily basis, I never achieved the level of softness that I felt as I ran my fingers along his scalp. The fine silk coverings on the bed were probably not as smooth, the pillows made of clouds not as soft.

I leaned down and stuffed my face into the back of his head, inhaled his scent and let the softness comfort me.

After a few minutes, far too soon in my opinion, he pulled

away and looked at me.

"I wish you could remember the number of times we spent our limited alone time in this very position, just enjoying the proximity and closeness of each other's comfort."

He looked so sad again, and my fingers were still entwined in the back of his head. I used that to pull him closer to me and kissed him.

There was no reason for me to kiss him, I just simply wanted to. Maybe I wanted to feel alive again, even if just for another second. Maybe he was just a good kisser. Or maybe I just wanted to comfort him any way I knew how. And I knew from our earlier kiss that it would be effective.

Regardless of the reason, I kissed him slow, and with as much passion and feeling as I could. I put my anger at the way my life had turned upside down, the fear of the unknown, the confusion that came along with it, the undeniable and unknown desire I had for this man, all of it went into that kiss.

His perfect lips and expert tongue matched me move for move, as if they knew exactly what to do and what to expect.

I wanted more. More kissing, more of him, more information. I just wanted more.

If this was a dream, which I still hoped it was, then what was the harm in going a little further? What could it hurt?

Why not lose myself in a dream with a handsome man that seemed to be absolutely perfect in every way, and unquestionably smitten with me? Well, perfect if you set aside the fact that he was incredibly crazy. Leave it to me to dream up a man in love with me that was probably clinically insane.

"No." He broke away from me and jumped up and away. He did not stop moving away from me to look back until he was at least ten feet away.

My lips burned from his kiss; my skin was on fire. Every muscle in my body ached the moment he pulled away. I felt like I needed him in order to take my next breath.

"We can't," he whimpered.

"Why not? According to you, I'm the queen, you're here to serve me."

"You can't be my queen any more if we make love. There are rules. We aren't allowed to be together." He was crying, his whole body showing tremor after tremor from his restraint. I wanted to wipe away those tears and kiss him again.

I got up from my seat and took a step toward him, he took a step back.

I could play that game.

He mirrored my movements precisely. Each attempt I made at gaining on him, he accounted for by adding exactly that much distance.

I smiled, because I knew where we were heading.

Just when he looked like he was about to catch on, the back of his knees hit the bed and he tumbled backwards.

I sprinted to meet him before he could find his way up and away from me. Without knowing how I knew it would work, I completely immobilized his mad scramble by simply placing one palm on his chest, the other on his cheek, and whispering his name.

Ryker, in turn, looked at me like I was the most magnificent creature he had ever had the pleasure of resting his eyes upon.

"Maddie, we can't," he pleaded again in a quiet, soft whisper.

I ignored him. My body was burning up and I was literally aching for him to touch me anywhere, everywhere.

I leaned over him and kissed his jaw softly, resulting in his whole body shuddering from anticipation and joy.

That was a satisfying reaction.

If I were awake, I would never be so bold. I would never be able to make such a move on someone, especially someone I barely knew.

But I was still convinced this was a dream. And when he kissed me, I felt alive. The further I went with him, the more awake I would become. And if it did not work, then it did not work. I felt deep in my bones that this would, at the very least, be a very pleasurable and much-needed experience.

Even in my dreamy state, I did not know what was coming over me. I felt like a girl possessed by desire and lust. I almost felt like I was not in control of my movements, that my maneuvers were being driven by a vacant need that nothing else could satisfy.

"Kiss me," I whispered with a heavy breath in his ear and then nipped lightly at his earlobe.

Ryker growled, low and sexy in his throat.

Within the next second I was on my back, and he was hovering over me, straddling me with his beautiful body.

He pulled his shirt from his body so viciously that it lay in shredded pieces all around us.

I did not care, it did not look like he did, either.

His breath was fast and hoarse, and I knew mine was too. After all, he was made just for me.

I looked at him. He was perfect. His chest was tanned and square, his stomach toned with a slight strip of manly hair leading down into the rim of his jeans. He was covered in battle scars. Some were only an inch long; others ran nearly the whole length of his chest all the way down his stomach.

Just looking at him made my heart pick up the pace and made

my palms sweat.

I moved my gaze from his chest to his face. He looked angry, vicious, dangerous, and sexy. He was glaring at me, eyes in slits, cheeks blazing a deep cherry red.

"Ryker." I reached up and touched a fingertip to the soft patch of skin below his bellybutton.

That seemed to be all the encouragement he needed.

His mouth was crushed to mine so hard it hurt, yet I wanted more. His rough, calloused hands were on the bare section of skin my shirt exposed when it rode up to my chest when he flipped me over, and he was grinding into me just enough so that I could feel the tight bulge underneath his zipper.

And then he was gone.

He was just gone. I opened eyes that I was not aware were closed, and gasped.

I was laying in my own bed, in my own dorm room. Gone were the amazingly velvety soft blankets, gone were the fluffy cloud pillows. And gone was Ryker.

CHAPTER 3

The rest of the day blurred by. Which made sense, because after my eventful morning with Ryker, I had passed out so hard, I did not think I would have woken up during a tornado. When I did wake up, it was already almost supper time. My stomach grumbled to confirm that I was indeed extremely hungry.

I debated calling Ally, but I knew she would be busy with her family. Even though she was the type of friend to answer her phone no matter where she was or who she was with, I did not want her to spend her weekend with her family talking to me.

I so desperately wanted to tell her that my dream self almost lost its virginity. She would want every detail. Now that I knew that it was all a dream, I was okay talking to her about it.

What other explanation was there for me to wake up in my own bed, completely aroused yet fully dressed, and completely alone?

And, realistically, what world would I have been in to have a gigantic room that was high up in the clouds yet could still see the people of far below?

Instead of calling Ally, I texted one of our other friends that we made on campus and told him to meet me at the dining hall for supper if he had not already eaten.

His response was almost immediate: *meet in ten.*

I ran a brush through my hair quickly and changed into a pair of torn and well-worn jeans and a simple black tank top. It had been incredibly hot all week and I knew it was going to be humid out.

I snuck a quick look in the mirror as I walked past and hastily decided on grabbing an elastic hairband for my hair and tossed it up without even looking at my reflection. There was no controlling these curls anyways.

I sprinted to the dining hall, even though I was nowhere near athletic. I had a lean body, but no skill to accompany it.

"Ouch." Tanner swung the door back open and looked at me. My friend had a tight grip on his nose with one hand and was rearranging his glasses back into their rightful position.

I had tried using the door to slow down my sprint, forgetting that it swung into the dining hall, not out. I must have bumped my friend right on the nose.

See, no skill.

"I'm sorry!" I laughed.

"It's okay, really." He was laughing too. We had both decided months ago that we were naturally born clumsy people. We were always bumping into people and falling over things that we should not have fallen over. It was one of the things that made us become fast friends. Ally took to him quickly, too. She said he was the male version of me, and therefore he was super lovable.

He was a nerdy type, with the big glasses and the short haircut. He was always reading and almost never had to study for any of his classes. It made both me and Ally jealous how smart he was. He was tall and thin, the typical kind of nerdy boy you would expect to see in a comic book store or sitting in a library poring over a stack of thick, old books.

Tanner casually slung his arm over my shoulders, and we walked like that all the way to the main entrance.

"Where were you all day?" he asked as he removed his arm and handed me a plate so that I could start dishing out my food.

"I must have been seriously tired or stressed," I mused. "I passed out hard after classes yesterday. I didn't even wake up until a minute or two before I texted you."

He looked at me, amused and shocked.

"Did you have any crazy dreams?" He waggled his brows, making me laugh.

"If you're asking if you were in them, no. You weren't." I tapped his arm and reached for the mashed potato scoop he was holding.

"A guy can dream," Tanner replied with a quick wink.

I used to find it odd how he would throw out random flirtatious vibes, but I had grown used to it.

Ally always poked fun at me and told me how she wished that Tanner and I would end up together some day. She would drone on and on about how scarily similar we were, and how adorable our kids would be. What she failed to realize was that opposites attract. I loved Tanner in a 'you're a great friend and I enjoy spending time with you' kind of way, and I was fairly certain the feeling was mutual at his end.

Besides, he sent out those vibes to everyone, including Ally. One of his favorite lines was about how he was lucky to become friends with the two most beautiful girls on campus, and how his dad would be proud of him to see us on either side of him all the time.

The truth was, if I had met Tanner a few years ago, I probably would have been absolutely flattered by his remarks. He would have been the kind of guy I would have wanted to go out with. He was smart, funny, cute in that geeky way. He was a total sweetheart.

But somewhere around the time I started my senior year of high school until now, my tastes changed.

I tended to be more attracted to the athletic type. There was something about a strong man with speed and agility that called to me. Again, opposites attract.

We sat down in a booth near the back corner of the dining hall. It was lit up a little dimmer than the rest of the hall since one of the light fixtures had burned out. It was a rarely visited section due to that reason alone. It had a ton of privacy, though. Naturally, Ally and I scoped that out first. It was actually where we met Tanner.

"Do you know what made you so tired that you slept for nearly a whole day?" he asked me around a mouth full of food.

"I think it's just stress. I have a few tests coming up, and I keep falling asleep in that philosophy class. I know my professor hates me; I know I am going to fail that course." I looked down at my plate, stomach grumbling, yet nothing on my plate looked appetizing.

"Are you okay?"

I looked up from my untouched food and looked at him. He was staring at me over the rims of his glasses, slowly chewing his dinner.

"Yeah, I just don't think I am that hungry."

Tanner shook his head and shoveled another forkful into his mouth.

"Just don't get too thin, you're beautiful just the way you are."

"Thank you." I smiled at him. It was such a Tanner thing of him to say. "What were you up to today?"

"Oh, you know." He flicked a fake piece of lint from his shoulder, putting on his masculine bravado. "Fighting crime, saving this campus, getting phone numbers. The usual."

I laughed louder than I intended to, causing the nearest few tables of students to turn and look at us.

"Come on, it wasn't that funny," he claimed. "I could have been out there mingling."

"With a book, maybe," I corrected for him. "Have you talked to Ally?"

I was missing my best friend something fierce. I needed to tell someone about the crazy long and super vivid dream I had, and I did not feel like Tanner should be the one to spill it to. Especially the part about the dream me almost losing her virginity to a fairy.

"Not really. I texted her a few times this morning, but that was it. She was already ready to get on the next plane and head back this way."

That sounded like her. Her family drove her nuts, they were always talking trash on the other side of her family and trying to get her to agree with them.

I made a mental note to text her when I got back to my dorm and check up on her. I did not need her going crazy too. I needed her to be sane long enough to hear my story.

"So?" Tanner's voice cut through my mental rambling. I realized he had been talking that whole time and I missed it completely.

"I'm sorry, what was that?"

"I was just asking if you wanted to watch a movie with me since Ally won't be back until morning. I can either go to your dorm or you can come to mine. I have a bunch of new films I have been dying to watch."

I really did not want to go over to his dorm. His roommate smelled like feet and had the odd habit of staring at me and Ally whenever we went over there. He never said a word to us, just sat there and looked at us, unblinking and unmoving.

I remember one day Ally asked him if he had a problem, he just smiled and kept staring. We later asked Tanner what was wrong with his roommate. All he told us was that he was here on some type of disability scholarship, that he was creepy but harmless and not to pay him much attention.

"You can come to mine; I'd rather not have to pretend to ignore Frankie."

"Sweet, any preference on snacks?"

I looked at my untouched plate of cold food.

"No, you can choose, I'm down for anything."

"All right. Well, I will meet you back at your dorm in—" He glanced at his wristwatch, and it looked like he was doing a quick mental calculation. "How about half an hour?"

"Sounds good."

Tanner got up, took his plate with him, and left the hall without another word.

I stared at the mashed potatoes, steamed broccoli, and chicken breast on my plate. It had smelled and looked so good when I first arrived here, now it looked like cold, dried out leftovers that get pitched because they've sat in the fridge for a week.

Pulling out my cellphone, I glanced at the time on my home screen. Ally would still be awake.

Just checking in. Have you gone mad yet? Hopefully not. Hurry back.

Her response was quick.

Girl, the fam is totally crazy! Ugh. Can't wait to get back. Flight should land around noon. Love you.

Well, at least she was still coherent enough to update me and let me know she was still chugging through. That was something.

I sighed and picked up my full plate, dumped its contents

into the trashcan and started to slowly make my way back to my dorm.

It really was turning out to be a nice evening.

The birds were out, the sun still shone bright and high in the clear blue sky. The campus was calm since most of the students were either in the dining hall eating or making their own microwavable meals in the privacy of their dorms. Only a few stragglers still mingled every block or two.

I was actually alone. I could take some time to rethink my dream, analyze it and try to figure out what it meant. Was I really just going crazy?

Ryker was not a hard thing to think about. I remembered him in excruciating detail. I could remember so vividly how he tasted, smelled, how it felt having all of his weight crushing down on me as he kissed me. I could still see the worry in his face, the desire behind his eyes. I could still feel the unreal softness that was his hair.

I also remembered that room. The room that excited and terrified me all at once. I remembered how odd the magnifying window was, how strangely beautiful the chandelier was as it hung from the ceiling and lit up the room.

I remembered every word those perfect lips had said to me, how each new piece of information made me feel.

I reached my dorm room way before I was ready. I had not even begun to dissect the dream; I was too stuck on Ryker and his amazing mouth.

"Hey!" Tanner came up behind me with his arms full of snacks. "I grabbed everything. We have popcorn, chips, snickers, red vines, and skittles because I know they're your favorite."

I smiled at my thoughtful friend and took some of the load out of his arms.

"I'll make the popcorn if you want to start the movie?" I offered.

He nodded and followed me into my dorm.

I almost tripped over myself. I thought I had seen someone standing in the middle of my room as I turned on the light, but I blinked, and the outline was gone. Tanner must not have seen it, or if he did, he did not say anything or show any signs of having seen anyone in the room.

It was probably just my overactive imagination. After sleeping for a whole day, stuck in a crazy dream, I could imagine my mind needed some time to relax and focus on something else, like the movie Tanner was popping out of its case.

A movie sounded like the perfect thing to take my mind off of everything. It would help pass the time, too, until Ally came home. She and I had spent many nights over the years where we would just forget the world and get lost in a movie. We had extended the movie night invitation to Tanner over the last few months, especially as we all became better and closer friends.

Feeling more optimistic, I grabbed the box of microwavable popcorn and made my way to the kitchen door. I opened it and walked through while reading the instructions on the box, closed the door and blindly walked towards the general vicinity of the microwave.

A hand grabbed my mouth, and I was pulled roughly back into someone. An arm enclosed around my middle, tightening me into whoever was holding me against them.

"Don't make a sound," the voice whispered into my ear.

It smelled strongly of mint.

I nodded as best as I could.

Ryker still held me pinned back into him and kept his hand clamped tightly over my mouth.

There was no possible way I was still dreaming, which meant I actually had a talk with a stranger about fairies, and I actually almost threw my virginity away to this man that I barely knew.

I did not care how attractive he was, what he claimed our supposed history was, or how turned on I became when he was near.

"I want you to get rid of him." His breath tickled my neck, and I had to work hard to suppress a full body shudder.

I was painfully aware that he was still proudly bulging in his jeans, and that he was pressed firmly at my backside.

"I will tell you later, after you get rid of him. He's dangerous, and I don't want him near you. I'm going to let you go, okay?"

I nodded, again.

His hand slowly eased off of my mouth and his grip loosened around my waist. I peeled away from him and glared at him over my shoulder.

Purposely, just to aggravate him, I grabbed a bag of popcorn from the box and shoved it into the microwave. I was not about to let him tell me what to do and act like he could control me. I would never, ever, be controlled by a man. Especially by a man I barely knew and was supposedly some mythical creature.

"That is not what I said to do," he seethed between clenched teeth.

I sensed he wanted to yell at me in frustration, or roar with rage at being defied.

I walked right up to him and leveled his glare with my own.

"I don't know who you think you are," I started. "But you will absolutely not tell me what to do or who I can hang out with. Tanner is not dangerous; he's a harmless boy and he wouldn't hurt a fly!" I jabbed a finger into his chest to drive my point home since I was not able to yell above a muted whisper.

Tanner was just in the next room, probably already finishing up getting the movie ready and setting up the rest of the snacks.

"You will listen to me. You know I won't let you put yourself in danger."

"Danger?" I was struggling to keep quiet. "What kind of danger could that sweet boy cause?"

"Just get rid of him. I'll come back when he's gone."

"If you think I want you to come back, you're crazy. I am not going to get rid of him just because you th—"

As much as I wanted to keep whisper shouting at him, I was cut short by him closing the inch of distance between us and clamping his mouth on mine, instantly melting away any anger or frustration I had with him.

It was a powerful kiss. Not like the sexy ones we had shared previously, or like the first one that made me feel alive in places and in ways I did not think possible. It was a kiss to prove dominance, control. It was a kiss to make me understand that he could easily get rid of Tanner himself, if he chose to. Because Ryker was big, and powerful, and strong.

"Get rid of him." He broke the kiss and then was gone before I could even catch my breath.

How was I supposed to tell Tanner to leave? Not that I wanted to. I felt like I did not have a choice in the matter, that Tanner could get hurt if I did not get him to leave. I did not want him to get hurt, especially by Ryker. Tanner did not deserve that.

Not that I wanted to think Ryker had the upper hand, because he did not, it would probably be for the best to reschedule with Tanner. I did not think I would have ever been able to forgive myself if anything happened to him because I was being stubborn and selfish, which I knew were two of my worst traits.

Still, it aggravated me to know that I was doing something only because someone else told me to. It was not fair to me or to Tanner. How on earth could Ryker say that Tanner was dangerous? I know I had not known Tanner for more than a few months, but he was probably the gentlest and most kindhearted guy I had ever met.

He was certainly more respectful than Ryker. All I got out of him was a constant hot and cold, in and out, stalker vibe that was accompanied by a lot of demands and glares.

"Tanner," I said as I walked into the main room of my dorm.

He was laying on the couch, a blanket over him with a bag of pretzels already open in his lap. I hated having to kick him out.

He looked up from the TV, inclined his head quickly in a 'what's up' kind of manner, and resumed his focus back to the screen.

"Any chance we could reschedule?" I let the question out quickly before I let my stubbornness kick in again.

Tanner looked up at me over the rim of his glasses, he looked hurt and rejected, and it made my heart sad.

"I just don't feel real well," I lied. "I started to smell the popcorn and it made me feel a little nauseous." I glanced over my shoulder to the door to the room I shared with Ally. "I just kind of want to lay down."

"Are you okay?" He got up from his comfortable seat and walked over to me, eyeing me up and down as if he would be able to detect whatever it was that had made me feel ill.

"Yeah," I tried to reassure him. "I'm just going to take some Tylenol and lay down for a little. Maybe we can have a movie weekend next weekend when Ally is home?" I suggested, trying my hardest to sound cheerful and optimistic.

"Okay." He sighed but turned away to start picking up

everything he had just lugged over here.

I felt so bad about making him leave. He was just trying to be a good friend, and here I was, lying to him and telling him to go. I was the lowest of the low.

"I could stay the night." He stopped what he was doing, back still turned to me, and froze in his place.

There was no way I had heard that right. Since when had Tanner ever wanted to stay over? I knew his roommate, Frankie, was a little weird. But Tanner seemed to be really good with him. I did not see any other reason he would want to stay.

"I could sleep in Ally's bed," he added quickly, still not turning around to look at me. "Or I could stay out here on the couch."

"Tanner, you can't stay the night. First, there's rules on campus about boys and girls staying in each other's dorm rooms after curfew. Second, I won't be much fun, anyways. I'll just be sleeping."

He turned around then and looked at me straight in my eyes. I did not think I ever saw such a serious look on his otherwise joyous and carefree face. He was almost always smiling, even when he was reading a new book his features were upturned and his eyes shined.

"I don't want to go."

"Why not?" I asked him.

He shook his head and looked down at his feet. I could see him taking a few breaths before he picked his head back up and looked at me again.

"To be honest, Maddie, I was going to make a move on you. It's no secret that I like you. Ally has been hinting at it for weeks now, trying to gauge if you liked me back because I'm way too chicken to just come out and tell you that you're absolutely beautiful." He stared at me the whole time he rapidly spoke, he did not even blink.

I had no words to say to him. The whole time Ally was making her comments and bringing him up all the time, I just thought that she was trying to play match maker. I never suspected that she had been talking with Tanner about me; I never imagined he actually liked me. To be honest, I never even contemplated liking him because I just figured we were friends, and that was all there ever would be.

"You don't have to say anything, really." He finally looked away.

I was glad he said that because I was not capable of words at the moment.

"I just..." He ran his hand through his hair and let out a long breath. "Is there a chance that we will ever be more than friends?"

I did not trust myself to speak yet. I did not want to hurt him, but I also did not want to lead him on and break his heart, either.

I shook my head once.

His face visibly fell, and I could tell I broke his heart anyways.

"I'm sorry." I did not know what else to say.

I could tell him that he was an incredibly attractive guy, or that any girl would be lucky to have him. But I did not think that would help any.

I could tell him that if I had known him longer, or if he had made his intentions clear in the beginning, that this conversation could possibly have a different outcome. I did not see that helping him either.

And while all of that was true, none of it would take the hurt out of his eyes or erase the frown from his lips.

If I had known him longer, there was a good chance I could

have grown deeper feelings for him. He really was a very attractive guy, with a brilliant mind, winning smile, and a romantic soul. He could have easily been the kind of guy I wanted to grow old with. Any girl would be extremely lucky to have him in her life.

I just did not want to be that girl.

I had no real reason why, but as soon as Tanner told me he liked me, Ryker invaded my thoughts.

I did not know Ryker at all. I had no reason to believe or trust him. I had no absolute way of knowing if he was real, or if he was still a figment of my overactive imagination.

But there was no way I could deny how drawn to him I was. I could not stop thinking about the way his hands on my body made my skin tingle, and his lips on mine made me breathless yet more full of life than I had ever felt. I could not deny the attraction I had to him that seemed much deeper than a day of knowing him.

As hard as it was to accept, I realized I was actually looking forward to seeing him again when Tanner left.

I wanted to hear more about this fairytale that made me feel special and painted me in such a good light. I did not believe it, but that did not mean I could not sit there and indulge in the thought of it.

"I'm just going to go." He grabbed everything and left quickly. I had nothing to say to make the situation better, so I just quietly watched him until the door was firmly latched behind him and he was gone.

Not even a second later, I sensed his presence behind me.

"I hated doing that," I confessed.

"I know." He reached around me, clasped his hands around my middle and leaned me back into him.

Just like that, I did not feel so bad. I did the right thing. It would have been a lot worse for him had I led him on or told him that there could be a chance for him and I to be more than just friends.

I still would not, and could not, believe the story that Ryker told me, but I knew deep in my bones that I would never be able to feel about anyone the way I felt about Ryker. The sad part about that was, I was not even entirely sure how I felt about him.

Was it love? If that was what this feeling was, could it be possible to fall in love with someone who was not even there?

I was a lot calmer when he touched me. He could talk for hours, and even though I would definitely interrupt him way more than I needed to, I felt as though I would enjoy listening to his every word, clinging to the story like the air I needed to survive.

"I feel you again." I could hear the smile in his words, even though I did not know what he meant.

It seemed silly to me that he was saying he could feel me again while his arms were firmly wrapped around me. Of course, he could feel me.

"Maddie," he whispered in my ear and slowly turned me around so that we were pressed chest to chest.

I looked up at him and immediately sucked in my breath. He was stunning.

His smile was huge and perfect. His eyes shone brighter than any star, and they glistened slightly as he held back tears. His sculpted cheeks were blushing a starburst pink. He was beautiful.

I could not help but smile back. He was pure joy, and it was infectious.

"I missed feeling you." He nuzzled into my neck and chuckled in my hair.

"What do you mean 'feeling me'?"

He pulled his head back and looked at me, I noticed one happy tear had managed to escape his eye despite the effort to hold them all back.

At least, I assumed it was a teardrop. It was not the normal clear drop that came from most people's eyes. The one making a wet track down his handsome, blushing cheek was a kaleidoscope or rainbow and sparkle.

"You're starting to believe, Maddie." He buried his face in the crook of my neck again.

I was having trouble following his words, especially with my focus being diverted to the feel of his warm breath skimming down my collarbone.

If I was going to figure out what he was trying to say, I needed to put some distance between us so we could both focus enough to communicate.

I pushed him away from me just enough so that we were not pressed into each other any more, but kept my fingers interlaced with his.

"Ryker, you need to explain a little bit, I'm not understanding what you mean."

"I'm sorry." He chucked again. "I'm just so happy, Maddie, I haven't felt you in so long."

"What does that mean?"

"It means, my Queen, that you are returning to me. You see, before your memory was erased, we were linked together by mind, body, and soul. We could feel each other's emotions, thoughts, locations. We were one, split into two." His face broke out into that ridiculously happy smile again. "I haven't felt you in a really long time. It was like a part of me was missing for a small eternity. But, I don't know why or how, I can feel you again. Not anywhere like how it used to be, it's more like an ember left after a statewide wildfire. But, Maddie, I feel you."

"Linked?" I asked him. I was hung up on that one word. How could you link yourself with someone else?

In some respects, I thought it would be incredibly cool to be able to locate your significant other, to hear their thoughts or feel their emotions. But I also felt like it was a huge invasion of privacy. What if I was going through some personal emotional turmoil, would he know about it? Or would I have to call out to him somehow in order for him to hear me or feel me?

Then I realized I was being crazy for thinking those thoughts. It would not matter how it worked, because he was just a lunatic with a cool story that had no sense of reality or validity in it. It was not like he would ever actually be able to know where I was all the time or be able to invade my thoughts.

"Yes, that's the best word to describe it. When I vowed to you, to love you and protect you forever, we were linked together, entwining our essences so that we were essentially two, made of one."

"Why would erasing my memories take that away, then? My memory has nothing to do with who I am, just what I know."

Ryker looked away from me, towards the front door of the dorm room that Tanner had just walked out of minutes before.

"We had to do a lot more than take away just your memories," he admitted, still staring at the door. "We had to change a lot of things about you, but all of it was to keep you safe, and all of it was agreed upon by you."

"Okay." Something about that bothered me. I felt like, even though it was just a story and not really anything that happened, I was fully invested in learning all about it. I was finding it more and more enjoyable to piece all the parts of the story together, even though I had barely begun sorting through the puzzle pieces. "If you had to do all of these things, these changes, and take away my memory to protect me, why are you coming to me now and trying to get me to remember?"

"That, my Queen, is a discussion we will have to have at another time. In short, you were in danger, and we needed to hide you. Now, our race is in danger, and we need you back."

"What kind of danger?"

He snapped his look away from the door and back in my direction and gave me his annoying analytical stare for a minute.

"You were in danger of being taken from us, and our race is in danger of dying out."

"This still makes no sense to me. What danger was I in? What was causing the danger? Is that danger gone now? Why would the race be dying out? What would me coming back do to save you?" The questions flew out of me; there was no stopping them once they started. I had so many more questions in me, I needed at least a few of them answered.

"There will be time for that, later. I promise." Ryker bowed his head to me. "But right now, I need to talk to you about that guy that was here."

"Tanner? What does he have to do with anything?"

"He is not the nice guy you think he is, Maddie. I feel he is a very dangerous guy and I really think you should stay away from him." Ryker grabbed my face with both hands pressed to either one of my cheeks and angled my head up so that I was looking straight into his eyes. "Please promise me you will stay away from him."

"How is he dangerous?" I could not promise to stay away from someone that had become a very good friend just because someone that showed up in my life a day ago asked me to.

"I can't tell you all of that right now. But I think he is part of the reason we had to change you. I don't think he knows who you are, or at least he isn't completely sure. But if he finds out, or if he is playing you, it could be very bad for you and for our race. I can't let anything happen to you."

It was insane that he was asking me to stay away from Tanner a few minutes after he told me that he liked me.

"Are you just jealous?" I asked. The thought that he would stoop so low as to make me stay away from my own friends because of jealousy made me want to laugh, but it was sort of a coincidence that mere minutes after Tanner said he wanted to move in on me, Ryker was flat out asking me to stay away from him.

"Of course not, my Queen." Ryker took one hand off my cheek and held it over his heart, feigning a look of hurt. "I have felt your pleasure and emotions as you bedded many men, I hold no jealousy for them, I certainly do not hold it for that man."

"But, if we are so 'in love'." I air quoted. "Why would you not be jealous of all of these men that I have supposedly slept with?"

I felt as though I brought up a valid point, and was actually looking forward to his response. I was getting really good at finding the loopholes in his story, and the better I was becoming at it the more I believed it was just a story.

"They may have your body," he said very seriously. "But none of them may have your heart. That was given to me, and I am the only man that may carry it."

"So, you're saying you aren't jealous of the men that get to have me, touch me, make love to me?" I egged him on. I was curious to see just how far I could push him.

His blush was back, I knew I was hitting the right buttons.

"I am not jealous of them. They are used for a purpose. Do I wish to know how you feel, how you smell, how you taste? Of course, I do, with every fiber of my being. I long for the day when I can make my love for you a physical intimacy shared by soul mates. But I know my place, I know yours, and I know you have basic needs and desires that I am not able to fulfil, the same as me."

I was pretty sure he was telling me that he went out and had a lot of sex, too, but I was not entirely sure.

I raised one brow at him and leaned away from him a little more.

The thought of another woman touching him, kissing him, enjoying him, made me extremely uncomfortable and irritable.

I had no reason to be jealous. I had only known this man for a day, and even if his story was impossibly true, I apparently had sex all the time, why should he not have the same freedoms and pleasures I did?

"Then why was it, again, that we could not be intimate with each other? I know you said there were rules. But if we can be intimate with other people, why could we not be intimate with each other?"

"That is hard to explain." He winced, as if he was struggling with something that was difficult to say.

"Try." Was my only response.

"Very well." He let go of me completely, then, and walked a few paces away to sit on the couch. Ryker placed his elbows on his knees and cradled his head for a moment. It looked like he was trying to build up his courage or organize his thoughts enough to say whatever it was he found so hard to say.

I gave him the space and time I could tell he needed, and remained where I was, standing where he had left me.

Finally, after what seemed like an eternity, he picked his head up and looked at me.

"Sex with me would kill you."

I could not help myself, I laughed loud and hard. There was no way sex with one man could kill me, it made no sense. How could sex kill anyone? It was not a dangerous thing to do, people did it all the time.

"Quit laughing, Maddie. It is a serious thing. Your death is not something to take lightly."

"I'm sorry." I laughed as I wiped away the stray tears from my eyes. "Ryker, how could it kill me? It's just sex, not that I don't think it's a big deal, because I do. But it can't kill you."

"My Queen, we are linked together. Which means that we feel everything the other feels. Making love with your soul mate, being that intimate and close with the one person you were meant to spend eternity with, well, there's no better feeling than that."

"And?" I urged him to continue.

"And, if I am feeling that satisfaction, and you are feeling that satisfaction, then we are not only feeling our own, but each other's at the same time. That would be far too intense for either of us to be able to handle. On top of that, it would cause the Spiral Effect."

"What's that?"

"The Spiral Effect is where you feel my emotions, which are the same as yours, so you are feeling them doubly intensified. If that alone does not kill you, then you will be sending that magnified feeling to me, adding that to my feeling, and I'll be sending all of that back to you, adding to you, and then you to me. We would never be able to get out of the distress of the never-ending feeling. If we did not die immediately, we would most certainly not survive the spiral effect, nobody ever has."

"Hence." I pieced it together. "The rules that are in place saying that we can't."

"Precisely."

"So, we just each go around having all this sex with whoever we want? That doesn't sound like love to me."

"The intimacy we share with others is how we agreed to refrain from intimacy between the two of us. We have the tendency to get carried away, sometimes. It is extremely difficult to simmer down on our own."

Theoretically, the things he had said made sense. It was a strange feeling, something finally making sense.

"But, if we can't feel each other right now, and I am apparently changed in whatever ways I was changed, what would there be to stop us now?" I knew I was testing the waters. I had no intention of being intimate with him, not now, or any time in the foreseeable future, at least. But if his theory of the Spiral Effect was actually accurate, then at this point there would be no danger of that happening.

"I have pondered the thought, I must admit." He looked down at his hands again. "I have desired you and wanted you for a millennium. I would be lying to you if I told you I did not want to try. But the risk of something going wrong still outweighs anything else. I must think of what's best for you, and what is best for our race. I can't be greedy, even though all I can think about is taking you and, finally, making you mine."

So, he was thinking about taking me. He was showing a great deal of self-restraint by keeping his distance in that area.

"But how come earlier we almost… you know?" I asked him, thinking far too vividly of his body pressed into mine, the feel of his throbbing bulge pulsing between my thighs with only the fabric of his jeans and my yoga pants separating us.

"We shouldn't have. I was being foolish in letting you get that close. I should never have let it go that far. I have no clue if it will kill you in the state you are in now, but I am not willing to try it. I need you, like people need air, but I need you alive even more than that. I won't let it happen again, my Queen. I am truly sorry."

It hurt my heart to see him looking so forlorn and talking so lowly of himself.

"Can I tell you a secret?" I asked as a way of trying to lighten the mood and cheer him up a little.

"Of course, you may always tell me anything."

"I kind of wanted to, earlier. I never have before. At least, not that I can remember. It would have been my first time, but I wanted to. I was kind of disappointed when I opened my eyes to see you and that beautiful room gone."

Ryker smiled at me, but it did not reach his eyes that time. It was a fake smile, plastered on a miserable soul. I could see right through it.

I wanted to see the smile from his heart again, it made me want to be happy too.

"It was hard for me to leave," he admitted. "Believe me. Every part of me wanted you, and I had never in my entire existence struggled so badly to leave it alone and walk away."

"You didn't walk." I laughed at him. "I blinked and you were just gone."

That made him chuckle softly, the smile that accompanied it was an easy, boyish grin.

It immediately made me smile.

"How do you move so fast?" I asked him.

"It isn't that I move fast, really." He got up off the couch and walked slowly towards me, both hands outstretched. His eyes locked on mine, and I could not look away, even if I wanted to, which I was not even sure if I wanted to any more. "Can I show you?"

I reached my hands out to meet his, not even giving it a second thought.

"All you have to do is think about where it is you want to go. It can be a place, a feeling or person. Every time I think of love or happiness, I am led straight to you."

I could feel myself blushing. I knew he could see it, too, when his easy grin turned into a full-on megawatt smile.

"Where do you want to go?" he whispered.

There were a lot of places I wanted to go. I would not object to going back to that giant, beautiful room that was supposedly mine. But there were some things that I felt were more important. For instance, even though I knew that Ally would be back in the morning, I would love to visit her. Seeing her would help me to confirm this was all reality and not something I made up in my mind after she left so that I would not feel so alone and bored.

I also really wanted to see the place where I was born but, seeing as how I had no clue where that was, and I was not sure how I felt about the whole situation, I could not go there, at least not very easily.

Oddly enough, I could not think of anywhere I wanted to be more than the here and now, with Ryker.

"I want to go to our favorite place." I finally decided.

I was immediately blown away with the electrifying, radiating excitement that showed in his beautiful face at my answer. I was instantly filled with joy and hope, and belief for a better future.

Happiness abruptly changed to shock, which made me feel lightheaded from the sudden drastic change in emotion.

"You felt me," he whispered, his tone echoed the shock I had felt skimming over my chest.

"Is that what that was?" I was amazed at how clear the feelings were. It seemed like they were my own.

"Yes." He kissed me slow and tenderly. "Are you ready to go to our happy place?" he whispered against my lips.

I could not think of the words to tell him, but I was pretty sure my happy place was wherever he was.

Instead of saying anything, I nodded once and allowed him to lead me.

"Think of peace, freedom; think of happiness and carefree love," Ryker directed me.

I did as he instructed, thinking with everything I could muster within me. I imagined quiet, because I was always at peace in the quiet. I pictured myself breaking free of chains and boundaries, imagined the ecstatic feeling that would surely follow after I finally freed myself. I struggled to think of love; All I could imagine was Ally and her sassy demeanor, her easy smile and beautiful face.

Before I heard Ryker's gasp, I felt the temperature change, it cooled a decent bit, but the chill felt delightful on my exposed arms. There was wind tousling the stray hairs that had fallen from my unruly bun. I could hear the birds and crickets all around me, and the distinct sound of tall grass swaying lazily in the breeze. It smelled like sunshine and outdoors.

I opened my eyes, and my own gasp mimicked the one Ryker gave.

We were standing in the middle of the most beautiful, cozy field I had ever seen. There was a line of trees that formed a perfect circle around us. It was a large area, but not so large that it was overwhelming. The grass was almost knee length and was littered with flowers of every shape, size, and color imaginable. I could practically smell each individual flower as the breeze wafted up their aromas. On one end of the field was an old-fashioned wooden swing that was lazily drifting back and forth in the wind. It had a canopy of the same beautiful flowers covering it, intertwined in the wooden slats. It almost looked like the swing had been sitting there for so long that the little flowers had been allowed to take decades to grow into the swing.

Directly in the center of the field was a giant blanket, set up with a picnic basket and champagne glasses.

There was absolutely nothing else in the enclosed area, but the simplicity and bareness of it only added to the intense beauty.

"I built this for you the night we joined our souls." He smiled at me though his lashes. "It was one of the happiest days of my life."

"This is such a beautiful place," I mused. "How often did we come here?"

"Not very often, unfortunately. Really, we could only slip away once in a while, and even then it became less frequent once we realized the danger that was looming."

Ryker laced his fingers with mine and led me to the blanket and picnic basket. Every step we took caused a bunch of butterflies to puff out of the ground. They were stunningly gorgeous. I had never seen such vibrant, exotic-looking butterflies before.

"What is this danger?" I did not want to ruin such a good mood, but he kept referring to this danger, and I had no clue what it was. How was I supposed to help my people if I did not know what the danger was?

I mean, his people. If there even were any people out there to help. It was just a story, after all.

"There is a king of another race of fairy that covets you and your position. He believes that by courting you, he can rise in station and power."

"I don't see how that puts me or anyone else in danger." I confessed.

"Well." He sat down on the blanket as we reached it and then pulled me down by the hand. I thought he was going to sit me next to him, but instead he sat me in his lap and held me. "You denied his proposal. This waged a war with him. The threat he has to you, the reason why we had to hide you, was because he planned on taking you. We got wind of his intentions through some of our spies, and it was not a pretty plan. He wanted to take you, erase your memories, and plant them with new ones where you were madly in love with him and accepted his proposal."

"That is not exactly a threat to me, though. I mean, not really. You erased my memories and replaced them with false ones. Didn't you?"

"In a way. I merely repressed your true memories and read you stories of what you now think of as your reality. He was going to destroy your memories, so there would have been no way of ever retrieving them. And then he planned on taking your power and killing you to claim his throne over both his and your people."

That did not sound good.

"Would it have been so bad if he ruled my people?"

He was quiet for a minute, and I listened to his heart beating under my ear as he held me.

"I'm not sure," he confessed. "But you knew in your heart that you did not want him leading your people, and I believe in you and your judgement without question. You have led us through so much already, and you have never been wrong."

I pondered that for a little. There were still so many things I did not know, so many questions that I wanted to ask. But I was feeling drained, possibly from the information overload, possibly from the serene surroundings.

"So, what is this place?" I needed a change of topic. I no longer wanted to hear any of the heavy, serious things our conversation had turned into.

"This." He smiled into my hair. "This is where we told each other that we loved one another, where we vowed to always love, honor, and protect. This is where we joined our souls."

I looked around again, taking in the amazing beauty and serenity that this place offered so freely. I could imagine having a wedding here, surrounded by the trees, walking on a flood of gorgeous flowers. The sun shining just right.

And, to me at least, he basically explained a wedding. Vowing to love and to hold, through sickness and in health, until death do us part. Two souls becoming one.

"So, who was it that said that we could not be together?" I had to ask him. The question had been floating in the back of my mind ever since he told me that we could not be together as long as he was my protector, and I was his queen.

He was quiet for so long after I asked the question, I was starting to wonder if I had not spoken it out loud at all, and instead just thought it again.

"There are forces out there, much greater than even your magnificent powers," he said, just as I was about to ask the question again. "They are responsible for keeping order to the world, the humans' and ours. If balances tip, it could result in the end of all life. They govern the laws, and we must abide by them."

"Or what?" I scoffed. "They'll track us down and kill us?"

"Yes," he replied instantly.

I had only been joking about the tracking us down and killing us thing. But it was good to know that I needed to abide by the laws that they created.

But, of course, there were no laws. Because there were no greater forces, and there was no race to save. I was not a fairy queen.

It was irritating that I had to keep reminding myself of this more and more.

"What does their law say, specifically, that prevents us from being together?" I whispered. I was not entirely sure I wanted to know the exact answer, but I wondered if there was a loophole around it that would possibly allow us to love the way we once did.

At least, according to his story, the way we once did. And that was if there was even really a 'him' telling me these stories. I still had not ruled out him being nothing more than a figment of my imagination.

"Well." He shifted beneath me.

I started to pull myself off of him, thinking that I had become too heavy, but he pulled me back down and hugged me into him once more.

"Technically we have broken the law by joining our souls. We have worked very hard to hide this from the public. That is another reason we must seek out others for pleasure. It helps to keep up the ruse that you are simply my queen, and I am simply your protector."

"Okay," I tried again. "But what does the law say that makes it so we can't be together?"

"It says that since you are a royal, you may only wed a royal. Joining souls is a lot more intense than being wed, but it is easier to hide. If anyone found out that we were joined, they would kill me immediately, and the loss of my soul would kill you." He spoke slowly, articulating each word as if he had to choose them carefully in order to help me understand.

There could essentially be a way around that law. I had no clue what it could be, but I was sure, given time, I could find it.

Theoretically speaking, of course.

"I know what you're thinking." I could hear the smile in his voice. "You're wondering if there is any way you can find to loophole the law. There is none, at least none that has ever been discovered before. It has been many millennia since the laws were set. If there were a loophole, I am sure someone would have discovered it by now."

"How did you know what I was thinking?"

"Because I feel you, again." He leaned back just enough so that he could look at me directly. "It's a little spotty, like when you have really bad cell service, but I can hear enough to make out the gist of what you are feeling and thinking. You are starting to believe me." He kissed my forehead.

The truth was, I did not know what I believed. I did not even know what I wanted to believe. On one hand, if I believed it, I would be powerful, respected, coveted. I would have found my soul mate and I could lead a whole race of people. However, I would also not be allowed to have my soul mate. That alone would be the hardest thing for me to be able to do. I would also have to be battling nonstop and have to become responsible.

On the other hand, if I did not believe any of this, I could go back to my normal life, at my normal college and take my normal classes with my normal friends. But I would also not know who my true love was, and I would always wonder if this dream rang any type of truth.

Living a life with no love, and constant wonder, that did not seem like the life I wanted to live.

"I want to believe," I finally confessed, more to myself than I did to him. "I just don't know how. Let's say this is all real, how could I get my memories back?"

His whole body stiffened, his brows drew together, and he shifted his gaze away from me and towards the swing on the one end of the field.

"Come on," I urged him. "You knew how to erase my memories; you should know how to give them back."

"I don't know. Nobody does," he whispered.

"What?" I was mortified. It seemed a great deal more than a little irresponsible to erase someone's memories without knowing how to repair them.

"Nobody knows how to retrieve them. We never had any intention of returning your memories. We needed to hide you and it seemed at the time like it would be indefinite. And only you knew how to erase them without deleting them completely. You created the spell we used to hide you, you did not have the time to create the reversal."

"But we are joined at soul, so wouldn't that mean that you know how I did it? If you know how I did it, then maybe we can figure out how to reverse it."

"That seems good in theory." He nodded. "But I have the feeling it isn't so simple."

"Why do I need my memories back so badly, anyways?"

"The king: he can't get your powers unless he kills you. He can't find you since we changed your genetic makeup, so he has decided to start killing off our people, one by one, until you come out of hiding."

"Wait!" I jumped off of him and began pacing circles around

the blanket he was still perched on. "So, in short, we hid me from this king who only wants my power and my people. He can only achieve that by killing me. But if I don't come out of hiding, he is going to kill our whole race slowly, but we have no idea how to change me back. So basically, I stay hidden and our race dies. Or, I figure out the impossible and restore my prior self and risk being killed for my power and people anyways?"

"Seems so." He sighed a long breath. "The worst part is, I have failed you. I was to protect you, and no matter what happens, it seems as though I was not able to. I was born for one duty, one purpose, and I could not fulfil it."

"There is one other option." I stopped pacing and stared off towards the swing that Ryker focused on earlier. I could practically imagine the wheels turning in my head, I was feeling confident about my plan.

"What is that?" he asked skeptically, not that I could blame him.

"We don't restore my queen self. I stay hidden. We use that to our advantage, we find him, and kill him before he even knows what's happening."

Ryker flew off the blanket and had his arms around me, kissing me repeatedly all over my face, giggling.

I had never heard a guy giggle before. It made me want to laugh too. I liked that.

"That is a brilliant plan, my Queen. Truly brilliant. We get rid of the problem and then focus on taking our time to reverse the spell and restore you to your prior glory."

There was only one thing I could think of to prevent us from pulling this off.

"How are we supposed to kill him if I don't have my powers?"

"Hmm," Ryker said. His face squished up and I knew he was thinking hard about something.

"It's possible," he said. "That we can train you in your powers. I don't know if it will work or not. But we were a lowly caste of fairy before you started to develop in your powers. It is possible that you can develop them again."

"I'm willing to try." I was willing. I wanted to try to do this the right way. If he thought that developing my powers was a possibility, I would give it my all. "I want to meet my people." I finally decided. It was time I committed, one way or the other. If I was going to believe this story, I needed to know more, I needed to know who I was protecting.

"Your wish, is my command, my Queen." He smiled and planted his lips softly on mine.

CHAPTER 4

Ryker reluctantly peeled his lips from mine, and when he did, I let my eyes slowly flutter open to see that I was in my bed chambers once again.

"This is my room," I whispered, more so to try to convince myself that this was indeed, my own room, that I had spent hours here, studying my subjects and plotting ways to help them over whatever obstacle they were facing.

"Yes," he whispered back. "Shall we look over them?" Ryker gestured with one hand to his side, towards the giant magnifying window.

I could not trust myself to speak, so I nodded and took a shaky step towards the wall of glass.

"Keep your mind open, my Queen. Try to believe in what you see, in who you are."

His words struck me as a little bit odd. Believe in what I see? What was I supposed to see? I had already looked through this very window, down at this very same village and seen my people. I merely wanted to study those I was destined to lead.

Three more steps to go until I was at the edge, and Ryker's voice penetrated through my thoughts, though I did not think I heard his words with my ears.

Believe, my Queen. Please believe.

I closed the distance, let my eyes adjust to the horrifying height, bright sun, and the optical illusion of standing so tall that I was level with the clouds, yet still able to clearly see every detail of far below me.

No warning from Ryker could have prepared me for what I saw. Even if Ryker had the good sense to describe to me in excruciating detail, I would not have believed what was before my eyes.

Surely this was not that same room, it was not the same window or the same village as earlier.

Surely this was all nothing more than a cruel joke.

"What do you see?" His minty breath was warm on my neck, it calmed me instantly.

"I see my people." That was all I could say to the brilliant sight.

Even though I could not remember them, my heart knew them. I had no idea my heart could remember someone that my brain did not. It was weird to me that I did not feel this way about the man whose soul I supposedly shared, but maybe your soul is different from your heart. Maybe that was why I felt so at ease with him, why even though he was telling me all these crazy things and whisking me away to unknown parts of the planet, I trusted him and allowed him.

But these people that I beheld so far below me, they were mine. I felt it in every bone in my body. They were mine, and I loved them more than I ever thought I could love.

Each person, that looked so normal the last time I had looked down upon them, now appeared completely different.

The kids playing in the street were not normal kids. They had the basic build and shape of a human, but they were covered in scales, and each child had different patterns and colors.

The woman that had been holding her child in the pool, well she was gorgeous. Her scales glittered in the sun, and her toddler definitely took after her likeness.

The fathers cooking on the grill were huge. The men were easily seven feet tall. Most of them had dark scales surrounding their mouths, with much lighter scales everywhere else, much like the way human men had their beards and mustaches.

Everyone was gorgeous, unique yet the same. And they were all mine.

"How come you don't look like them?" I asked Ryker, not able to look away from them to him.

"I do, kind of." He brushed his arm up against mine as he came to join my side at the window, visibly relaxing at knowing that I could finally see them for who they actually were. "I have the power of disguise; I can wear many skins and appear differently to different people. You can think of it as shape shifting, though I am limited to human-like living creatures."

Finally, I was able to tear my gaze away from my people so far below me to look at Ryker, trying to see past the disguise that he wore. I was dying to know what he truly looked like. Would he be colorful, or would he be plain and simple? Would his scales glisten in the light or shine a metallic glow no matter where he stood?

No matter what he truly looked like, I felt in my heart that he would be stunning.

"You won't be able to see through it." He laughed at me: a full belly laugh that made me laugh as well.

I loved his laugh. I loved the way his smile reached his eyes, deepening the sparkle that was always glistening there. I loved the musical way his chuckle lifted my spirits and made me feel like I was wrapped in a warm, comforting embrace.

His smile eventually died; his laugh ceased. He stared at me for a long moment as my laugh finally sizzled out, too.

"I feel you." His words sounded like he was speaking around

a throat full of gravel. "I feel you falling in love with me."

I still was not sure how this soul sharing worked, or how much of my thoughts and feelings he could feel, exactly. But it was a little unnerving and intimidating to know he knew what I was feeling before I even knew what I was feeling.

And why was I already feeling that? I had known the guy for less than two days – had it really only been yesterday we bumped into each other?

"Don't be frightened, my Queen." Ryker wrapped his arms of serenity around my frigid body, and I instantly melted into him, suddenly no longer concerned that things were moving alarmingly fast. "I can turn it off, it's like a light switch. I can turn off my ability to tune into you, and you can switch off your ability to tune into me. If you aren't ready for all of this, I will willingly turn off the switch. It's just that I haven't felt you in so long, I did not want to turn it off."

I had to give that some thought. There could be some benefit to having him keep the switch on. For instance, if I was confused or overwhelmed, something I was not very likely to admit to him, he would know and probably be able to calibrate the speed and immensity of the information being thrown at me.

However, I felt like there was a lot more that I wanted to keep to myself. I had not even figured out my own thought process on all of this, yet he knew where I was. I would never admit to him, or anyone else, that I was developing feelings for him. Even though it would be impossible not to fall for him.

His handsome, perfectly sculpted features, the broad muscular shoulders that moved so fluidly under his t-shirt...

"You're doing it again." He smiled his lopsided boyish grin.

"Sorry." I was not sure if I was really sorry. Then again, he probably already knew that. "Keep it on. I think there may be more benefit to you knowing what's going on in my head than not."

"I would be happy to keep it on." His boyish grin turned into a full smile that made his eyes shine brighter than the sun that hardly seemed more than ten feet away.

"Just don't comment on it so much. I don't think I'm ready for that yet, and it's a little weird being constantly reminded that you can basically read my thoughts."

"Oh, I can't read your thoughts." He turned serious. "I can project my thoughts to you, but I can only hear what you want me to hear. Only if you are thinking loudly enough can I hear what is going on in that beautiful mind of yours."

I knew his calling me beautiful had made me blush, but I could not help it. All of my life I had thought of myself as just average, which was the biggest reason I loved Ally so much. She represented everything that I felt like I was lacking.

She was smiley and bubbly, perky and bright. I was dark and dull. She had beautiful bouncy hair, and mine was a mass of untamable curls that never wanted to have a good day. She was athletic and beautiful. I was lean and long. We were complete opposites but complimented each other in every aspect.

"Maddie." It was the first time Ryker had said my name in what seemed like forever, pretty much since the moment he started referring to me as his queen. "You need to know just how beautiful you truly are. I wish there was a way for me to show you how I see you."

That was an interesting concept. Not that I cared to see myself as beautiful, I had long ago accepted myself for who I was, even if I did not like it.

But Ryker claimed that if I thought something loud enough, or projected a thought to him, he could hear me. Well, I was supposed to be practicing my 'powers', so would it not make sense to try to practice accepting a thought, or perhaps an image?

"Could you try to project to me how you see me?" I was skeptical, I was not even sure if images were something that could be projected between two fairies with joined souls. But I supposed I would not know if I did not ask.

"That is a fantastic idea!" Ryker was practically vibrating from his excitement at the prospect of starting my training.

I must admit, I was pretty excited, too.

"I'm going to try to show you, in detail, exactly how you appear to me, everything I find beautiful about you. Now, you may look different than what you are expecting, because I still see you as my queen." He braced his hands on either of my shoulders. "Are you ready?"

I nodded, not even sure how I could possibly be ready for something like this.

Nonetheless, I closed my eyes and opened my mind. I let everything from the past day pour into me, all of the knowledge, sights, my people from far below me. I threw in all the fear I was feeling from the crushing responsibility I did not yet want to own up to. I let everything out on the table.

"Turn your mind off, my Queen," he whispered so close to my ear. I had not felt or heard him move closer to me.

Doing as he asked, I pushed everything aside and thought of him, and him only. I did not think about the unknown, or the burden of being a leader. I cast away the feeling of guilt at having abandoned my people. I refused to let the shame and hurt of not being with my love enter my mind.

I simply thought of the man standing in front of me. I felt his fingers grazing my arms lovingly as he tried to soothe me. I felt the comforting magic of his love flow through me.

And then there I was.

I looked nothing like I did when I saw myself in a mirror, yet I knew it was me.

The brilliant golden scales, those were mine. The glittering tail covered in deadly sharp thorns, I used that in battle. The toned, built frame of the clearly powerful woman, it was all me. I wore a crown of shimmering emerald upon my golden head. My hair was well past my knees and was close to brushing my ankles. There was not a single curl to it. Every inch of me was golden, adorned with a strategically placed emerald green scale.

The beautiful fairy pictured in my mind was beyond gorgeous. She represented everything strong, courageous, worthy. She exuded great wisdom and power. She walked and talked gracefully and confidently.

"I'm beautiful." I was awed at how stunning I was as a fairy, and every bit of me yearned to be that radiant version of myself.

"My Queen, your belief grows stronger every moment. You are growing stronger with it." He kissed each of my eyelids with soft, tender care.

I opened my eyes and looked at him, and my breath caught in my throat.

He had silently dropped his own human disguise.

I was right in my original assumption. He was absolutely stunning.

Ryker was tall, taller even than the men in my village. He was nearing eight feet tall and was twice as wide as he was with his disguise. His muscles bulged everywhere; I did not think there was an inch of him that was not heavily strengthened. His scales were midnight black, with a hint of blue in the direct sunlight. He was magnificent to look at. The most mesmerizing thing about him, though, were his eyes.

They remained the same electric blue and stood out so vividly against his dark coloring. They pierced right into me.

His hair, I was shocked to realize, was the exact same color as his amazing eyes, and fell just below his shoulder blades.

"Was it too soon?" he whispered.

"No, not at all." He was gorgeous, even more so in his true form. Which was absurd since I was technically human. "Maybe," I admitted. I should not have found him attractive in his true form. My genetic makeup was currently not fairy. And humans and fairies, I doubted they mixed.

His scales quickly melted before my eyes, his body shrank back into the size I was familiar with, his muscles squeezed into one another. Within the span of two blinks, he was back into the same Ryker that had caused me to drop my books yesterday.

I could not believe it was only yesterday all of this had begun. It had to be near Sunday morning by now, surely, I should be back in my dorm room to greet Ally.

Was it possible for me to simply go back to my dorm room, though? How was I supposed to put on a nonchalant façade and pretend my life was not currently hanging by an overly taut thread, along with my sanity?

Ally would know right away that something had changed. She knew me like no other person ever had or ever would.

The thought of never seeing her again broke my heart. There was no way I could stand to just up and leave her without any type of explanation.

"She won't believe you, my Queen." Ryker brought me back from my thoughts.

He was probably right. I still did not entirely believe what was happening, either. But I also could not keep pretending it was not really happening. I wish I had time to figure everything out.

I knew there was no time, though, as much as I wanted there to be.

I was torn between living two lives, each one was enticing and exciting, but I knew I could not have both.

I needed to make up my mind, come to a conclusion and follow it through.

"Take me to my dorm, please."

A small part of me regretted saying the words as soon as they passed through my lips. It made me feel sick to my stomach to leave this room, to walk away from the view of my people below me, to not stay and look at the immaculate beauty everywhere. I wanted to get my memories back, and I knew deep in my bones that I would only get them back while I was here, in my own land.

But I needed to go. I needed to return to my college campus, be with my friends and go about my life.

The weekend was almost over, and so was this fantasy.

Ryker visibly crumpled in on himself. His shoulders hunched together, the corners of his mouth dropped, and he looked down at his feet.

I knew I was hurting him, and even if I did not want to admit it, it hurt me to know I was disappointing him.

"I need to go." It was all I could think of to say.

He nodded his drooping head, hugged me into his chest and held me tightly for a moment.

When he let go, I was back in my dorm.

My heart hurt to look at him any longer, I definitely did not want to say goodbye.

Instead of trying to form the words that my heart knew but my mind could not process, I opted for walking away from him, going through the bedroom door, and closing it behind me, hoping with all my might that he would get the point and leave.

There was no time to wonder if he picked up on my cues, I had work to do, and not much time to do it.

Before I could forget a single detail, I grabbed my notebook, that I never used in class, and a pen that for some reason never made it into my pocket before leaving the dorm and began to ferociously write everything that was said and seen over the last day.

I quickly became lost in reliving it all. Each moment that came and went was vivid and full of life. I could feel all over again the shock and surprise, the love and the hurt, the anger and confusion. It was as if it was all happening again.

Before I knew it, I had filled up the entire notebook, not a single page left untouched. There were a few entries where I had attempted to draw something, like the magnificent bed, or Ryker. Or Ryker on the magnificent bed.

Fortunately enough for me, I was not a very good artist. The drawings could barely be made out as anything other than hastily scribbled lines and eraser marks. I knew what they were though.

When the entire notebook was filled up, I grabbed another, and then another. Each one I felt was barely enough to contain all the details and images that were fighting in my mind.

Eventually, I passed out on my notebooks. The information that took over a day to enter my mind was finally pushed out, fast and without a break. It exhausted my body, mind, and soul.

CHAPTER 5

"Wakey wakey!"

For the second time in less than forty-eight hours, I was jolted awake by my best friend.

This time, however, instead of waking up to realize I had slept through a whole class, I woke up crumpled on my desk, a sheet of notebook paper suctioned to my cheek from the puddle of drool that had escaped my open mouth.

I slowly picked up my throbbing head off the desktop, rubbed a hand on the back of my stiff neck, and turned around to look at my best friend. It felt like a whole lifetime since I had last seen her.

I was up and out of my seat, squealing before she even finished materializing in my peripheral vision.

She was in my arms, and I was perfectly aware that I was thoroughly crushing her.

"Calm down." She giggled in her musical voice. "I haven't been gone that long."

Ally pried my arms from around her and took a step back.

"You look like crap," she said, ever so bluntly. Which was really the only way Ally ever said anything.

"Thanks!" I was giddy from having my best friend back. I did not care that she just insulted me. She was back.

"What's going on? I've left for the weekend many times." She was giving me an odd look; I would probably be doing the same thing if I was in her shoes.

Of the many times she had left, I could not recall a single one where I ever hugged her when she returned.

"Nothing, it was just a long weekend, that's all." I dropped my arms to my sides and just smiled. I was so happy to see her!

She raised one of her perfectly symmetrical brows in an obvious look of skepticism and used her natural born dramatic maneuvers to bob her head from side to side as she looked past my shoulder and to the contents of the top of my desk.

When she saw the notebooks, her features evened out in a very serious kind of manner and she cut her glance back at me.

"You actually studied?" The shock in her gasped reply was both extremely understandable, and slightly hurtful.

"I can study! But no." I glanced back at my desk, still unsure if I should be telling her anything.

But if anyone could help me through something, it was her. I knew without a doubt that I would not regret telling her. I would only feel bad about the dumbstruck look she would give me and the fact that I was giving her something she could endlessly make fun of me for.

It was now or never.

I picked up the first of my filled notebooks, clutched it to my chest and tried so desperately to convey a look of pleading and truth to her with my eyes, to tell her that I was trying to be serious, and it was not the time for jokes.

She just nodded and held out her hand.

I knew she would pick up on my cues, she always did. It was a completely different story if she listened to them and followed them.

Ally grabbed the notebook from my hands before I had fully convinced myself I was doing the right thing and could hand it to her myself.

With no choice but to sit and wait patiently, I watched her as she scanned a few pages, her eyes rapidly moving left to right repeatedly.

Each time she flipped over to a new page my heart skipped another beat.

Was I being incredibly foolish? I was handing her this detailed inventory of my entire weekend, with no clue what to even make of it myself. What would she think? What would she say?

I held my breath, waiting for her to say something, or at the very least, make some type of expression on her blank face.

Just when I thought I was going to pass out from lack of oxygen, she sharply tore away from the pages in her hand and narrowed her eyes at me.

She still had not said anything, but I could practically see the wheels turning in her head. I knew she was trying to figure out how to tell me I was crazy without actually saying those words.

Eventually, her features relaxed back into their usual calm and collected selves.

"What is this?" she asked cheerily, the way I hoped she would.

"What do you think it is?" I wanted to hear her thoughts before I told her it was a detailed account of my weekend without her so that I had more reason to tell her that she was never allowed to leave me alone again.

"I'm not sure." Ally looked back at the notebook, and then towards the desk where three other notebooks sat. "What are those?"

"The rest of the story." I shrugged. I figured that was the best way to describe it to her. It was a story to anyone who was not me.

To me, it was a confusing long, horrible, exciting weekend.

"So, it's a story," she said.

I did not answer. It seemed like she was asking me, confirming that was all it was, but she did not say it like a question. She asked it as a statement, and I did not know if I needed or wanted to answer right now.

Ally handed the notebook back to me and smiled her happy smile.

"It's good. I didn't know you wanted to be a writer. To be honest, I didn't think you were that creative."

"Okay." I laughed. "You've been back for five minutes; can you not insult me so much right after you get back?"

"Sorry." She slung her arm over me. "I'm starving. Wanna go grab breakfast and I can tell you all about my glamorous weekend?"

"You're always so hungry!" I swung my arm around her, and we headed towards the door.

"You need to change first." Ally crinkled her nose at me. "You don't stink, but you can definitely tell those aren't clean clothes. You have a very…" She used her other hand to waft the air in front of her, turning the moment into a dramatic one. "Earthy scent." She finally decided on.

"I'll change. Be right back."

I headed for my closet and, for the first time in a few very long days, felt like everything was going to be okay.

So what if I did not tell Ally that everything I wrote down actually happened? I would get to it, eventually.

Baby steps.

For now, her having read some of it and not calling me insane was enough for me.

I finished changing and walked out of my closet and back

into the bedroom. Ally had chosen to sit in the chair at my desk while she waited and was looking at the notebooks sitting there. She was not touching them, just looking at them. Her back was to me so I could not see her facial expression.

"Ready?" I must have startled her because she jumped almost a foot out of my chair and spun around quickly.

"Wow, you dressed fast." She walked up to me, put her arm over my shoulders again, and sniffed dramatically. "That's better! I texted Tanner while you were changing. He's going to meet up with us."

Tanner? Surely, he did not fill Ally in on the embarrassing moment the other night. I did not think he would want to relive that again, and quite frankly, neither did I.

"Okay," was all I said, even though my brain was screaming the same word over and over again.

Danger.

But Tanner was not dangerous. He was a sweet guy. I was not sure who Ryker thought he was, but he had to be wrong. I had become really close with Tanner, and if he was even a little dangerous, I would know.

Still, the warning bells were ringing, and my palms began to sweat. That one word roiled around continuously, boiling over until that was the only thing I could think of.

I did not dare voice any of this to Ally. She would definitely think I was insane if I did.

Ryker was wrong, he had to be. I had spent many times alone with Tanner. If he was dangerous, I imagine he would have tried to hurt me, or at least slipped up a little bit by now.

No, Tanner was harmless. I was sure of it.

We approached the dining hall, and I was immediately relieved to see that my friend was standing outside, waving, and smiling his natural friendly smile.

Tanner reached out to hug Ally as we closed the distance between us and him.

"How was the trip?" he asked Ally.

I knew she would eat that up. I had not even asked her how her trip was.

As much as I loved her, I could freely admit that she was the rich, spoiled conceited type. It probably hurt her a great deal that I had not bothered to ask.

"It was great, thanks for asking. I will tell you all about it when we get settled down." Ally held the door open for me and Tanner.

We had an awkward moment as we simultaneously gestured for the other to walk through first.

"Am I missing something here?" Ally said as she eyed us both suspiciously. "Did something happen while I was gone?"

"No," he and I both said in unison.

His cheeks turned a bright ruby, and I knew mine were not too far off from matching his.

I could feel my face burning as I remembered the other night when he came over.

"Okay, well I just thought of something new I want to talk about while we eat." She gestured with her head for us to both go through the door she was still patiently holding open for us.

I did not even look at Tanner. I just started walking for the door, which turned out to be a huge mistake.

He had to have had the same thought process because he did the same thing.

We collided into each other, side by side, as we both moved to go through the door at the same time.

"I'm sorry," he muttered as his hands flew out to

automatically catch me before I completely lost my balance and fell on my butt in front of everyone.

"I'm sorry. I should have looked at where I was going." I held onto his forearm for support until I could feel the ground beneath my feet again.

"It's okay." He smiled with his dorky glasses falling halfway down his nose. "I don't mind holding you like this."

"Oh, shut up and help me get back on my feet." I laughed and pinched his arm where I was gripping onto him.

And just like that, all weirdness between us faded. We were friends again, laughing at each other and poking fun. The way that harmless, not dangerous friends do.

We walked the rest of the way through the hall, over the rows of food and to our normal seat in the rear of the dining hall with the dim lighting.

It felt good to have a normal morning breakfast with my friends.

I was starting to relax a little, sitting there with Tanner across from me and Ally next to me. My eggs were scorching hot, my bacon was nice and crispy, and my oatmeal smelled of heavenly cinnamon and honey.

"So," Ally started, around a forkful of her own steaming eggs. "Are you two in love or what?"

I almost spit out my mouthful of oatmeal, but instead started choking on it because I foolishly gasped at the same time.

Tanner was behind me and was frantically patting my back. I finally got the food dislodged from my throat and chugged half of my glass of milk to soothe my throat and catch my breath.

"Why would you even ask that?" I finally managed to ask.

"Well, the way you are both being so awkward around each other, and the way Tanner practically flew to help you out just now…"

"She was choking!" Tanner sat back down in his seat across from us. "You think I won't help my friend when she's choking?"

Ally looked back and forth between me and Tanner.

"No, something's up." She looked Tanner square in the eyes. "Spill." It was such a simple demand but, coming from Ally, it carried a lot of weight.

"I told her I had a crush on her. That's all," he admitted with his hands up in submission.

She swiveled on me so fast, I almost started choking on my next bite of oatmeal, too.

"What did you say?" She smacked me hard once in the center of my back to dislodge the food before it became fully stuck, again.

"Thank you," I croaked through my increasingly sore throat. After I caught my breath and had a small coughing fit, I could finally answer her. "Nothing, just that I was happy being friends and wasn't interested in more."

"I can't believe you like Maddie!" Ally said to Tanner.

He remained quiet but smiled at his food and shook his head.

"What?" she asked.

"She knows you know." He looked at her over the rim of his dorky glasses.

"Oh." Ally shrugged and went back to her own food. "Well, guess the cat's out of the bag now. So, what do you think, Maddie? Wanna be his girlfriend?"

For the third time in a row, my food involuntarily stuck in my throat.

Tanner, again, came to my rescue and helped me until I had dislodged my bite and could breathe. After he finished patting my back, he rubbed small circles between my shoulder blades until I could quit coughing and had levelled out my breathing.

I pushed my plate away from me, no longer hungry. My throat was too sore now, anyways.

"As I told Tanner, I only want to be friends."

"But, why? He's such a cutie, and he's smart and funny."

"Then you date him."

"Uh, 'him' is standing right here." He plopped back into his chair. "And 'him' doesn't feel very good about two attractive girls fighting about who should not be dating me. Besides, it's only a crush. It's no secret that Maddie is beautiful. I don't want to hide the crush any more. Anyone would be lucky to date her. I hope she finds someone who will make her as happy as I know she will make them."

Tanner stood back up, grabbed his plate, and left without another word.

"Geesh." Ally looked after him. "What's his problem?"

Truthfully, I wanted to follow Tanner. I felt bad that he was put on the spot like that. I knew he was still embarrassed about being turned down; anyone would be. And I really thought that Ally was way out of line.

"You are." I hated being harsh to her, but I hated how she chased him off even more. "That was uncalled for. You didn't have to badger him about how he feels. Nobody likes to be pressured, Ally."

I did not even give her the chance to respond. I was furious with her, and I could probably count how many times I was unhappy with her on one hand since the day we had met.

Angrily, I snatched up my plate of uneaten food, dumped its contents in the trash bin and raced to catch up with Tanner.

Ally might not see how she was in the wrong, and she might not apologize. But I would. It was unfair how she pushed him when he was obviously uncomfortable and embarrassed over the whole ordeal. I knew I was embarrassed for him.

"Tanner!" I shouted when I saw him on the sidewalk a block in front of me.

He stopped and turned towards me. It looked like he wanted to turn back around and keep walking, but instead he stood there and waited while I jogged clumsily up to meet him.

"I'm really not in the mood, Maddie," he said when I was only a few steps away.

"I just wanted to say I'm sorry," I said between heavy huffs of air as I tried to catch my breath. "I think she was out of line, I'm sorry."

He did not say anything, he merely nodded his head once and looked off to his side, clearly trying to not look at me.

"Where are you headed?" I was desperately wanting to forget everything and just be friends again. I wanted to leave his confession in the past, and I really wanted to leave Ally and her snobby attitude behind.

He looked at me then, and I instantly felt bad. His eyes were red, it looked like he was struggling to hold back tears.

Had my rejection hurt him that much? Or was it the way Ally was acting all pushy?

"What is it?" I asked him. I wanted to reach out and pat his back, rub his arm, something to let him know I was there for him. But I also felt like touching him would not be the thing he would want from someone who just turned him down.

"I just don't get it." He shrugged his shoulders, and his glasses were starting to fog up from the humid morning. "I don't get why you won't give me a chance. Am I that bad?"

"Absolutely not!" I shouted. I realized I was loud and hasty enough that some other students passing by looked at us. "I just don't think I want a relationship is all," I said a lot more quietly.

"One date?"

It seemed a lot like he was begging, and I really did not like that. The red in his eyes was intensifying, and his cheeks were starting to match them.

He was definitely putting himself out there, asking me again after I said no the first time. I had to give it to him, the boy was persistent. And he really was a sweet guy. Could one date really hurt? I did not want to lead him on, but I also did not want to hurt him. There really was no good way to go about answering him. It seemed like no matter how I answered him, he would end up hurt one away or another.

"Never mind." He turned and took a step away from me.

"Wait." I grabbed his arm and spun him back around so that he was facing me. "One date."

His whole demeanor changed, his face lit up, his cheeks brightened, and he was suddenly standing two inches taller.

"Really?" He turned to face me fully, eyes glowing with a smile that reached his ears.

"Yes, but only one date." I could not believe I was agreeing to a date with Tanner. I really had no interest in anything other than remaining friends with him. "Don't tell Ally," I hastily added. It seemed like a horrible idea to let Ally have the satisfaction of thinking she was right after how pushy and rude she had been. She was already a pushy person. Giving her any reason to think that it worked in her getting what she wanted could easily spell disaster for everyone else.

"Done!" He giggled, he actually giggled. "Where would you want to go? What would you want to do?"

"Well, I mean, we don't have to figure that out right now, in the middle of a campus walkway, do we?"

His face fell a little, but he was clearly still happy that I had even agreed to a date.

"Okay, you're right." He took a step back. "So, to answer your question, I am not really headed anywhere. I was thinking about going down to the campus pond and sitting for a while. It's a nice morning and it calms me down to listen to the water." Tanner took in a breath to continue but held it for a moment as if he was debating saying what had popped into his head. "Would you care to join?" He held out his hand.

Now would have been the perfect time to tell him I was headed the other way. Or that I should go back and find Ally before she could cause any more trouble.

I took his hand.

Why did I take his hand?

We walked like that without saying a single word to each other, across campus to the small pond that students were normally sitting by to study, eat their lunches or just relax.

That morning, the pond was completely empty. I did not even hear a bird in the sky above us.

Tanner led us to one of the benches on the far side of the pond. That was fine by me, I preferred the far side of the pond. There was enough sunlight that you could bask in the heat, with a bunch of trees close by in case you decided you wanted a little shade to cool off in. And for the most part, the students always chose the side of the pond closer to the main road.

Ally thought it was strange of me to prefer the solitude of the far side, but I also preferred the corner of the dining hall that was ill lit and scarcely had other students in it.

I was just a loner and liked having a little bit of privacy. It was not exactly like privacy was something I had a lot of while living on a college campus with my best friend as my roommate.

I had tried keeping a journal when we first came here, but I soon figured out that Ally knew no boundaries and I quickly became very tired of having to constantly find new hiding spots for the absurd thing. Besides, I usually ended up telling her everything eventually, anyways.

"Hello?" Tanner was waving a hand in front of my face and looking at me like I had magically sprouted ten more eyeballs.

Which, with my weekend, I was not sure was entirely impossible.

"I'm sorry, I kind of got lost in thought," I admitted to him. "What were you saying?"

"I was just saying that it's a nice morning out. I asked you if you had anything planned for today."

"Oh. No, not that I can think of. You?"

"No." He concentrated on the pond for a moment, and I caught him in his poor attempt at looking at me from the corner of his eye. "Want our date to be tonight?"

That was tricky. On one hand, I could get it done and over with and then this whole thing could be done and over with. On the other, I was not so sure I was ready to fulfil the obligation of one date with Tanner.

"What did you have in mind?" I was skeptical. Maybe he had thought of something spectacular on the way down here, and it would not sound so bad after all.

"Well," he began. "I was thinking about having a picnic down here at the lake, maybe around eight? I can have everything packed up and set up so all you have to do is arrive."

That did not sound too bad. Eating food by the pond like I had done dozens of times with him and Ally. I would not have to cook then either. It would also be a good break from the dining hall food.

"That's fine." I finally decided. At least it was something innocent, it was not some huge romantic thing. I was honestly a little worried he would try to woo me and win me over with some gigantic gesture full of romance and 'love'.

Maybe a date with him would not be so bad, after all.

"Great!" He jumped up off the bench and held out his hands for me to follow suit.

"I think I am going to sit here for a little bit." I had just gotten there, and now that I was sitting down there, the breeze cooling my sun-warmed skin, the sound of the pond bubbling as the fish jumped and swam lazily, I wanted to stay and relax for a little.

I did not realize how wound up I had become over the weekend until I was sitting down, actually relaxing for the first time.

"No problem. Just don't forget. Want me to swing by your dorm to get you, or just meet you down here?"

"I'll just meet you here," I may have said a little too quickly. "I don't want Ally asking a bunch of questions until she absolutely has to know."

"Are you going to tell her at all?" He looked hurt all over again.

I could not win with this guy.

"Of course," I told him. "After the date. I just don't want her thinking she was in the right for being so pushy. And I would rather know what exactly I should tell her before I tell her anything."

"I get it." He smiled. "You want to tell her the date was spectacular and that you fell madly in love with me before she gets in your head."

I could not help but smile at that. It was an absurd thing to say, and he knew it. He was aware of the fact that I did not see him as more than a friend, I had made that perfectly clear. He knew I only agreed to one date to make him happy. He had to understand that. There could be no way he really believed I would fall in love with him, especially after only one little date.

"No, I really do get it." His smile dimmed a little, but his eyes still shone brightly. "I'll see you at eight!" He turned and sprinted gracefully off towards the main campus and away from me.

That was kind of weird. We were both really clumsy people. That was one of the reasons we became such good friends in the first place. I did not think I had ever seen him run at all, and there he was, running up a steep hill all the way to the main campus at full speed like it was nothing.

I could jog a block or so, but that was nothing compared to how he was scaling the hill as though he had mastered the skill years ago. If I attempted to run the way he was, I would have probably fallen after five feet and slid down another ten on my stomach, leaving grass stains on my clothes and dirt clumped in my unruly hair.

Then again, now that I was watching him, I could see that he had bulked up quite a bit. I wondered briefly if he had been working out as a way to impress me, but I quickly dismissed that thought.

It made no difference to me what his motives were, or even if he was in fact working out. But it was a little unsettling to see how he was up and over the hill in less than two minutes when a month ago it would have been easily a five-minute run.

Regardless, it was none of my business and I did not feel like spending all of my much-needed alone time to ponder over things that did not matter to me.

The sun was shining through the branches above me just

enough to make my skin feel warm without me starting to sweat. No doubt the breeze cast off by the fountain in the middle of the pond helped to keep the heat at bay.

It was a beautiful morning, and I was incredibly happy to get the chance to enjoy some of it by myself, alone with just my thoughts, sitting in the sun surrounded by a beautiful scene, rustling leaves from the trees around me, and the calming bubbling from the fish a few feet away.

Times like this did not come to me very often. Between classes, studying, eating, and being dragged off to every event by Ally or Tanner, I was almost never able to enjoy some solitude.

"Are you really going to go with him?"

The voice behind me made me jump and shattered the restful state I had only just begun to enjoy.

I turned to find the source of the voice even though I already knew who was behind me and really did not need to look.

It was the only person capable of moving through the noisy grass without making a single sound. And I had started to suspect that I would know his voice anywhere.

"He isn't dangerous," I told Ryker.

He looked gorgeous in the morning sun. Ryker wore a simple pair of blue jeans that looked worn in and faded to almost white in some spots. His plain red t-shirt stuck out among the green grass and clear blue sky. The breeze brushed the ends of his hair lazily above his shoulders.

As much as I wanted to enjoy my solitude, I wanted to be with him more. And as silly as it sounded, I felt like I could enjoy solitude much more if he was next to me.

"You're still going out with him." Ryker was beautiful even when he was clearly sad.

"It's only one date, and it's only to get him to stop asking and leave it alone." I hated knowing that I had upset him. It was not my intention at all to make Ryker sad or jealous. My only goal was to get Tanner to realize that I was not who he wanted so he could put his silly crush to rest.

"I know you don't feel anything for him, I know that." He finally reached me at the bench and sat next to me. "But it doesn't make seeing you with him any easier."

I could see where he was coming from. Even though I had not known Ryker long at all, and barely knew anything about him, I felt as though my heart would simply shatter if I saw him with another woman, no matter what the circumstances were.

"I'm sorry." I meant it. I was angry at myself for putting him in that position. I never wanted to hurt him and seeing him so sad made me sad. "It'll be over after tonight. I would cancel, but I'm sure he's already blabbed to Ally even though I told him not to. And I can't handle Ally when she is in her inquisition mood."

Ryker just nodded and put his arm around me like we were old friends. I could not help but notice how he did not get too close. It almost seemed like he was intentionally leaving a few inches between us. His whole body was rigid, like he was under great strain.

"What's wrong?" I asked him.

"I just don't want you to go. But you are my queen. I have seen you in the arms of many, I can handle one more."

"I won't be in his arms!" I scoffed. The fact that he thought that I was that easy to seduce really upset me. Just because as my 'queen' self I indulged a little, did not mean that who I was now would be the same way.

"Just please be careful. I beg of you, Maddie." He looked at me, every feature on his handsome face set in stone. "I would not be able to live with myself if something happened to you."

He was being way overly dramatic. Nothing was going to happen to me because Tanner was not dangerous. The idea of him being a danger to me at all was highly laughable. He was a sweet guy, with innocent intentions. And in any case, we were only having a simple dinner, right here on campus where there were thousands of students and staff all the time. Nothing would happen.

"Can you tell me about you?" I wanted to change the subject.

His quizzical glance made me realize just how drastic the change was, but I had realized I did not know much about him. Since the moment we met he had done nothing but tell me of myself. All I knew about him was that he was my protector, he was made for me, we shared a soul, and that his name was Ryker. I wanted to know more, I wanted to know everything if I could.

"Please?" I asked sweetly, putting on what I hoped passed as an innocent smile.

Whatever goofy look I had on, it worked, because his scrunched-up eyes relaxed, and a moment later his body did too. He was back to giving me that boyish half grin, and he pulled me closer to him.

"There really isn't much to tell." He shrugged. "I am approximately one hundred and four years old. My—"

"What?" I interrupted him. "If you were made for me and you're that old, how old am I?"

"Ah, my Queen. Your beauty never ages."

"Shut up!" I laughed and playfully smacked his hard stomach. "How old am I, really?"

"Nobody knows for certain. You were part of the original lower caste of fairy. You guessed your age to be eighty-seven when you started your rise to power. Since you've claimed your stake at the throne, four hundred and thirty-three years have passed."

Not having ever really been good at math, I tried to calculate that in my mind. Ryker was extremely patient while I took my time. He sat there and let me do my thing and come to the conclusion on my own.

"I'm five hundred and twenty years old?" How on earth could he expect me to believe that?

"Give or take a decade or two," he confirmed.

"Why were you made for me when I was so old?" I asked him. It made no sense to me that he would have been made over three hundred years after I had come to power.

"There were other protectors before me," he said. "They either failed you and were disposed of, or they died fighting for you. There were seven born protectors before me. I am your eighth and, if I can help it, will be your last."

"Were you made, or born?" He had said several times that he was made for me, and now he said that I had seven born protectors before him.

"Both. It's kind of a confusing thing to explain. You know how humans breed dogs for certain things? Well, fairies breed fairies as well. Kind of. We breed magic within the fairy. My mother and father were two exemplary specimens, both excelled in strength, fighting and magic. You had used some of your magic while I was in the womb to give me an extra dose of courage and bravery. I was born and could wield a sword before I could even speak five words. I grew up learning from you, from all the warriors in the village, and taking in all of the knowledge I could. I was born already in love with you."

That was a lot to process.

"I was born, but I was made to protect you. Falling in love, and you returning the feelings, that was all unplanned." He touched my jaw with one finger of the hand not wrapped around me. "And I would never, ever trade it for anything in the world. Your love has been even more fuel to the fire I have inside of me to protect you with everything I have."

Oh, yeah. He was good. His words made me melt from the inside out. He definitely had no worries about Tanner. I did not think I could ever feel for someone the way I felt for Ryker. Not that I could ever admit that to anyone. Being madly in love with someone you had not even known for forty-eight hours sounded crazy no matter who you were.

"Can I kiss you?" he whispered. He was so close to kissing me anyways, and I had no reason to say no.

I closed the distance between our lips and let him kiss me.

I would say that butterflies fluttered in my stomach, but that was not nearly accurate enough. It was a feeling closer to a firework finale.

"Wow," I said breathlessly when he ended the kiss.

"Yeah." He was equally out of breath. "I have to remember that we can't, even though I want to. And I can't risk putting you in danger."

I had heard that enough times to know that he had his foot planted down solidly on the issue. Which was fine by me. I was a virgin, and I planned on staying one for quite a while longer.

At least, this version of me was still a virgin.

This whole thing was still so confusing.

"Tell me more about yourself." I wanted to know him inside and out, but I also wanted a distraction from the thoughts racing through my mind about his body.

"Um…" He let out a long puff of air. "I have fourteen brothers. Each one is in your army, but I oversee all of them. I have led eleven battles and won eleven battles. My favorite pastime is staying with you in our meadow. My favorite pastime without you would be painting. It's the one thing about me that has nothing to do with war and protection or being born or bred."

"Are you any good?" I asked him, genuinely interested.

"I've had a little bit of time to perfect my technique. Some would say no, others would say that I excel. It all depends on who is viewing my work. Which, honestly, has not been many."

"I would love to see your work." I was being completely honest. As someone who was not athletic, or academically advanced, art in any form was a deep love of mine. I was very passionate about the things that I drew or painted.

"I would be honored for you to come to my painting room. As my queen, you have never stepped foot in there, or even known that painting was a hobby of mine."

"Why not?" I asked him. I was appalled to hear that I would not take an interest in his life if he was my soul mate.

"Don't be upset, Maddie. You had no way of knowing. I never willingly shared that part of my life with you."

"Why?"

"There is no real reason." He shrugged one of his giant shoulders. "I guess I just did not want to appear to be less of a man. Seeing you in the arms of so many who aren't me, I wanted to be as masculine as possible so that you would not stray your eyes from me for too long."

"Then why tell me now?"

"Because you either hopefully won't remember any of this when your memories are restored, or it won't matter because they never will be."

"Do you think I will get my memories back?" I was afraid to ask the question, I was even more afraid of what his answer would be.

"To be honest, I am not sure." I could tell that he was being truthful. He really had no idea if I would ever remember the past or who I really was. I could also see that he was terrified because of that. "But I have to stay hopeful that you will. Each day that passes without you remembering, more and more of our people are being slaughtered. I must stay hopeful that you will remember."

Talk about pressure.

What I would never admit to anyone, was that I was conflicted on if I even wanted to remember. I felt like I had taken the right step in deciding to believe that all of this was possible. But remembering also meant that I had a lot of weight on my shoulders. I was responsible for a whole race of fairy, and I was not so sure I could do that and be that person for them. But I also knew that if I never remembered, I could never help my people in the way that they needed to be helped, and then their deaths would be on my hands.

It was a difficult situation no matter how I looked at it.

"Maddie."

I tore my gaze from the lake to face him. His tone was serious.

"I want you to remember who you are for a lot of different reasons. Some of them are selfish, and some aren't. But I know I need to help you remember, because not wanting you to remember goes against everything that I was made to do. I would not be protecting you if I kept you in the dark on what has been happening to your people. That would not be doing you any justice."

I tossed his words around, trying to figure out what exactly it was that I wanted. I wanted to feel in my heart the answer, but I only saw a blank slate. There was no sign telling me what to do, there was no instruction manual explaining how it all worked. I was lost. I had a strange feeling of being incredibly small in an immensely large world.

It was terrifying.

"Go on your date tonight, Maddie. But please be careful. I don't yet trust my ability to find you in case something goes wrong. I will go to the ends of the earth to keep you safe, and to help you remember if that is what you wish. I trust you and will love and support you no matter what you choose."

He kissed me again, long and slow. I wanted to memorize the feel of his mouth just as much as he seemed to want to memorize the feel of mine.

I committed to memory the vanilla and mint scent with the subtle sweet cherry mixed in, his stubble chafing along my chin and cheeks as he kissed me.

Then his lips were gone, I opened my eyes, and so was he.

The solitude that was so sought after barely ten minutes ago, now made me feel more alone than I had ever felt.

Well, I supposed it was time to get up and start my day. I had a date to prepare for, and I was positive I would have an interrogation more intense than the Spanish inquisition from Ally.

I could hold off on that though. It would be easy to take my time walking to my dorm. At a regular pace, I could get there in about ten minutes from the pond. That could easily be dragged out to fifteen or twenty if I took my time and leisurely strolled along the lengthier paths.

I took one last glance at the pond that was still completely empty of all students. It gave me an eerie chill.

Then again, making it to the safety of my dorm quickly could not hurt either.

I attempted to sprint up the hill, much like the way that Tanner had. I fell far more gracefully than I ran, numerous times. It probably took me at least ten minutes just to make it to the top of the hill. By the time I reached the main road, I was far too tired and sore to keep running.

That was okay, though. Because I could see dozens of students milling around, completely unaware of what had taken place less than a quarter mile away from them over the steep hill.

Still, it was far too weird of a morning for me to not take at least a brisk walk back to the dorm.

"Thanks for ditching me!" Ally screamed as soon as I had walked through the door. I had not even closed it fully behind me yet before her attack began. "I've been back for a total of five minutes before you run and ditch me for your new boyfriend. That's low, Maddie."

"I didn't ditch you. I knew you hurt his feelings and I wanted to make sure he was okay." I finished closing the door behind me and turned to face her. "And he isn't my boyfriend," I hastily added.

"Whatever." She flopped down on our couch and swung her legs up on the coffee table. "We didn't even get to talk about my trip!"

She droned on and on about how her trip went. She went into elaborate detail on the flights, the food she ate, the people she talked to and the drama that inevitably unfolded over her weekend.

I zoned her out, giving the supportive nod and smile every once in a while to convince her that I was actually listening.

There was way too much on my mind to care about such menial and materialistic things.

For instance, I had a date with someone that my soul mate

was convinced was dangerous, meanwhile I had less than a day to decide if I wanted to be responsible for leading a whole race of fairies, or if I wanted to be responsible for their death.

Being a college girl no longer seemed easy and fun.

"Hello?" Ally cut into my thoughts. "What are you doing later? I have some sleep to catch up on. But I want to go out for dinner. Any suggestions?"

"I actually have plans. A study night."

"With Tanner?" She leaned forward in her seat and her eyes lit up.

"He's helping me out in a couple of classes, the way friends do. Nothing else." I plopped down in the seat next to her. "Now go to sleep."

"You are so boring!" She got up and sauntered off towards the bedroom. "Night!" she flung behind her shoulder and then she was gone.

I had no clue what I was going to do for—

I snuck a glance at the clock on the wall and gasped. It was already after two in the afternoon. I had six hours before I was to meet Tanner down by the pond. Where was the time going?

The last few days flew by, the time vanishing faster than I could have imagined it would. Yet it managed to feel like it dragged on, which left me even more tired.

I could just close my eyes for a few minutes, clear my head and try to sort through the tumble of information and garbage that cluttered it.

I could relax, in the safety of my own dorm, with the solitude I had so desperately wanted earlier.

It would all be okay, eventually.

CHAPTER 6

"Hey," a voice whispered to me, cutting through my dream.

My eyes fluttered open, and my vision blurred as I strained to get the sleep from my eyes.

"Hey, Maddie." A hand was on my shoulder, shaking me. "You fell asleep."

I used both hands to rub my throbbing eyes and looked up at the person talking to me.

Tanner was standing there, crouching over me whispering.

"Ally is still asleep; she doesn't know I'm here. Let's go before she wakes up."

He grabbed my hand and hoisted me to my feet.

"How long was I asleep for?" I whispered back. I did not want Ally to come out here to find me and Tanner in the dark living room.

"I'm not sure," he said. "But it is almost nine. I waited by the pond for you, and when you didn't show up or answer your phone, I figured I would come check on you."

"I am so sorry!" I was completely mortified. I could not remember a single time in my life I had ever slept so much. And now I had overslept and made Tanner think I had stood him up.

"It's okay, really." Tanner handed me a duffel bag. "I took the liberty of picking out some clothes for you, change quickly and meet me out in the hallway."

He did not wait for a reply, he just quietly and quickly made an exit, shutting the dorm room door softly behind him.

I wanted to tell him that I was too tired to go anywhere. I wanted to say that it was too late, and that I was not even hungry.

But with no other choice since he had already left, I took the bag into the bathroom to change since I did not want to wake Ally up in the bedroom.

I peeked inside the duffel bag and saw that it was a really nice outfit that Tanner had picked out for me. It was not something I would have picked for myself, but it was gorgeous, nonetheless.

I had no idea where he got the clothes from, though, or how he knew what size I was. Maybe he was just really good at guessing. And he seemed like the kind of guy that had a lot of different connections. He honestly probably got all of the information from Ally. It did seem like the kind of outfit she would put together, and she knew what size I wore.

After hastily putting on the ensemble, I checked myself out in the mirror.

Not bad.

He had given me a black blouse that was loose fitting and covered in millions of midnight blue sparkles. It reminded me of Ryker. It shimmered the same dark blue that his scales did. The pants were just simple black jeans. It looked really good on me, and I was surprised with how flattering the design was on me.

With no clue what to do with my hair, I took one of Ally's clips that looked like a sparkly blue and green butterfly and used it to clip the left side of my hair back behind my ear.

Good enough.

I also borrowed Ally's plain black ballet flats to complete the look.

I almost never wore much black other than the occasional shirt here and there, I found it was too dreary. But I was definitely feeling good in the outfit that had been chosen for me.

Maybe I should just have Tanner pick out all of my clothes. Maybe the two of us did not have a future together as a couple, but I could at least look good with his help in shopping.

I rushed from the bathroom as quietly as I could, tiptoed to the door and crept out of the dorm room.

"Wow, Maddie, you look incredible." Tanner grabbed my hand and span me around in a full circle so that he could see the finished product of his handiwork.

"Thank you." I was completely embarrassed that he could choose better outfits than I could, and absolutely mortified that I was actually going through with this date.

"Seriously. And doesn't it feel kind of good to be sneaking out?" Tanner waggled his brows at me and gave me an 'inside joke' kind of look.

"We aren't sneaking out," I chastised. "We are just going to the pond to eat. Nothing more."

"Did you tell Ally?" he asked me as he grabbed my hand and led me down the hall and away from my dorm.

"No," I confessed. "I told her we had plans, but I told her that it was a study session, and you were helping me in some of my classes."

"Ahh," he mocked. "So, you lied to her, and then snuck out. You really are a bad girl, aren't you?"

I was starting to feel extremely uneasy with the way he was talking. He was not sounding like the Tanner that I had become good and fast friends with.

Maybe he was just acting weird because he was nervous for the date. I knew a lot of people who got like that. And it was possible I was not acting weird because I had no feelings for him whatsoever.

I opted to not respond to him at all, hoping he would get the subtle hint and quit being weird.

"I'm sorry," Tanner said. "I'm just nervous."

It was like he read my thoughts. Which was impossible.

"It's okay. Let's just act and talk like we do every day, as friends." I felt like I had to clarify.

"Okay, then." He was silent a moment. "You look very pretty, Maddie. I am glad that you agreed to do this."

"That's better."

We exited the dorm building and the cool air from the lowering sun was a stark difference from the much warmer building we had just exited.

"Are you cold?" Tanner asked.

He started to shrug off his jacket and had it wrapped around my shoulders before I could tell him that I was not really cold and that I would quickly get used to the temperature change.

"Thank you," I said instead.

We walked the rest of the way to the pond in silence. There were very few students around, and I wondered why some people were up and about so late. Not that a little after nine was late, per se, it was just late for me. I was a morning bird and preferred to be in bed by nine most nights.

As we approached the top of the hill that sloped down to the pond, he asked me to close my eyes.

With much hesitation and little time to debate and weigh the pros and cons, I obliged.

Tanner took his time in guiding me down the steep hill, step by step, until at last it felt like I was on even ground again.

"Open them," he whispered very close to my ear. His warm breath on my neck gave me chills.

I did as he instructed. I opened my eyes and was absolutely

amazed at what I saw.

In the few hours since I had seen Tanner, he had completely decorated the perimeter of the pond.

There were stakes in the ground circling the entire body of water, stringing from stake to stake were gorgeous mini white lights. They sparkled in the rippling water and made it look like the top of the pond was covered in dancing stars.

He had woven a bunch of flowers through the lights and had a bunch more strewn around the ground.

There was a giant, deep, wine-colored blanket a few feet away from the pond. On it sat a wicker picnic basket, two wine glasses and one flickering candle.

It was the most romantic and beautiful scene I had ever laid my eyes on in person. It looked like it came straight from one of the hopeless romantic movies that Ally always had me watch with her.

I gulped. I was in big trouble.

"Tanner," I started. I had no idea how I was going to break it to him that I was completely unaware just exactly what his intentions were. "I think you have the wrong idea about this date."

"No. I have one shot to wow you; I plan on doing this the right way." He grabbed my hand again and walked me to the blanket. "Are you hungry?"

I allowed him to guide me into a sitting position on the blanket. Not because I was being wooed, but because I realized just how starving I actually was. I could not remember the last time I had eaten, and whatever was in that picnic basket smelled divine.

Tanner smiled the same easy, relaxed smile that I was used to seeing on him. It helped me to relax a little. But only a little.

I could not help but notice his hands shaking a little when he opened up the picnic basket and pulled out what he had prepared for us.

I barked out a quick laugh before I could stop myself.

"I wanted to make your favorites; I knew I should have gone with something fancier." He stared down at the plate, clearly disappointed in himself and the choices he had made.

"That's not it at all," I reassured him. "It's just that I was expecting something fancier, but I am super happy and relieved that you didn't make some elaborate thing."

I grabbed my plate from him and inspected my food closer.

He had nailed it; it was my absolute favorite foods.

Grilled cheese with pickles, and tater tots topped with nacho cheese and bacon. It looked and smelled perfect.

"Really?" he asked skeptically. "You aren't just saying that to make me feel better?"

"Really," I said around a giant mouthful of gooey grilled cheese. I could not help myself. I was starving. "This is absolutely perfect."

Tanner relaxed some, and then grabbed his own plate.

I noticed he barely ate; I assume it was from the nerves. He also seemed to struggle to look at me. Probably because I had cheese and bacon all over my face and was not the most attractive date ever. But that was okay, I did not want to be.

With my belly full, I set down my plate and licked my fingers clean from the cheese, savoring the taste.

"That was delicious, thank you."

"You're welcome." Tanner set down his own plate of half-eaten food.

"Are you not hungry?" I asked him.

"I'm just a little nervous," he confessed. "I really like you.

And in that outfit, in this setting, you are gorgeous. You look like a fallen star."

Even in the rapidly fading light I could clearly see the blush starting to creep up his cheeks. It was kind of cute.

"There is no pressure tonight," I reminded him. "You don't need to woo me. This date was honestly pretty good. I didn't know what to expect, but it definitely wasn't this."

"Well, it isn't over yet," Tanner said excitedly. "But, out of curiosity, if it were over, would it have been a good enough date to go on another one with me?"

I smiled at his easy canter and how relaxed he had become.

"Are you kidding me?" I joked with him. "Grilled cheese and tater tots? I'd go on a dozen more dates like this."

Tanner lit up, his whole face was enthusiastic, and he straightened up another inch, clearly very pleased with himself.

"Anyways, like I said, the date isn't over yet."

He reached back into the picnic basket and rummaged around a little.

I grew impatient sitting there waiting to see what he was going to pull out.

"What else is there?" I asked, not wanting to wait any longer.

"Ahh." He started to pull his hands back out of the basket. "Here it is."

His knuckles cleared the top of the basket.

I tried to look at what he had pulled out, but it was covered in a towel. Tanner looked at me over the rim of his glasses, smiled a little, and started to slowly unwrap the towel to reveal its contents.

Finally unwrapped, I could see that it was a box.

The suspense was killing me.

Tanner handed me the box and motioned for me to open it.

I could not help myself, I felt like a small child on Christmas morning.

I tore off the top of the box and looked inside.

"What is this?" I stared at the inside of the box.

"It's for you."

I ripped my gaze from the gift to face Tanner. I was puzzled.

Inside was the most beautiful charm bracelet I had ever seen. It was silver and sparkled like the reflection of the lights in the water. It housed at least two dozen charms.

Except, every charm was a different fairy.

"Why?" I could feel my heart pounding harder and harder, and I was convinced it would either break through my chest or just stop completely.

"Well." Tanner took the box gently from my hands and slowly pulled out the bracelet. "I bought it for you a while ago, honestly. I thought about giving it to you for your birthday next month. Ally helped me pick it out. But when you agreed to go on a date with me, I figured that would be a nice time to give it to you."

"But that doesn't say why you picked this bracelet."

He had been reaching out to me to put the bracelet on my wrist but paused in his attempt and dropped his hands in his lap as he thought about how to respond.

"I don't really know," he said eventually. "I saw it sparkling in the display, and I thought it was beautiful. The fairies are all different colors, and they shine. It was unique and pretty, like you. And like I said, Ally helped me pick it out. She agreed that you would love it."

Did he know? How would he know? Was he really dangerous, like Ryker had warned?

No. It had to be just a coincidence. Maybe he really did just think it was a pretty piece of jewelry that reminded him of me. And if Ally helped him pick it out, then clearly it was not all on him.

What if Ally knew, too?

That was even more absurd. I had shown her the notebooks I wrote in, and she thought I was just writing a book.

They did not know. I was sure of that.

I was getting worked up for absolutely nothing.

I tried calming my shaking nerves and thundering heart, I picked up my hand and held it out to him so he could put the bracelet on me.

He did, carefully, not even brushing my skin with the tips of his fingers as he did so.

I took a closer look at the bracelet when it was firmly clasped onto my wrist.

It really was beautiful.

Unlike the fairies that I had seen the other day, these were like the ones in books and on TV that resembled Tinkerbell.

In fact, there was even one that was probably supposed to be her.

It was just a coincidence.

"Thank you, it's lovely." I put my hand down and looked at him. "But you really didn't have to get me anything."

"Like I said." He shrugged both shoulders nonchalantly. "It was originally for your birthday. I just changed when I was giving it to you."

"Well, thank you." I smiled at him. My heart had calmed down a little. I was able to breathe a little easier.

"No problem." Tanner looked uncomfortable all of a sudden. "Would you maybe, I mean, if it isn't too much, uh…"

"Spit it out." I laughed.

"Would you maybe want to dance, with me?"

"There's no music."

He reached into the picnic basket and pulled out his iPod and music dock.

I regretted saying that as my reasoning not to dance with him. Not that it was him I was rejecting, it was the dancing.

"You know I can't dance," I protested. "I can barely keep my feet under me while walking, what makes you think I can dance?"

"I will lead you."

He did not let me object a third time. He had the music playing and had me up and onto my feet within a second.

With no choice but to roll with it, I allowed him to lead me in a dance.

Tanner had picked a slow song that I had never heard before. It was all instrumental, and the sounds tinkled and chimed in perfect rhythm.

With that particular, beautiful song, and with him leading the dance, for the first time in my life I felt graceful.

I realized what I must have looked like to him. A dark and shimmery girl, dancing through a brilliantly lit romantic scene with a boy that was fairly easy on the eyes.

I knew if anyone was watching, they would think I was a girl in love.

At that moment, I did not care.

I was too busy enjoying the feeling of floating on air, of feeling graceful and beautiful and loved.

I felt free and happy, spinning through the air, being held by two strong arms, even if they were not the arms I wanted to be swaying with.

I smiled and laughed, letting the music flow around and through me.

Too soon, the song ended.

I was out of breath from laughing so much.

I opened my eyes to see that he was still holding me, a lot closer than I thought he was. He was still spinning us around, slowly.

I looked at him, he looked at me.

Carefully, not breaking eye contact, he lowered his head to mine and touched our foreheads together.

I stared into his eyes, and he stared into mine.

"I was going to kiss you," he confessed. "But I just want to look at you. I don't think I have ever seen you look so happy, so carefree. You are mesmerizing, Maddie."

I could not respond. I refused to.

Because the only thing that was on my mind was how I wanted him to kiss me, and how disappointed I was that he did not.

That was absurd. I had no feelings for Tanner. He was a great guy, and he was smart and attractive. But I had no feelings for him.

I instantly felt guilty for thinking about how his lips would feel and taste.

I had Ryker. And even though I did not know what to say about him, and I could not define who we were together, he was still very much in my life. And I felt very strongly for him. I had no business kissing, or wanting to kiss, anyone else. Especially someone that Ryker was convinced was dangerous.

I was awful.

"I'm sorry," I whispered and pulled away from him quickly.

His smile disappeared, and his eyes narrowed in confusion.

"What is it? Did I say something wrong?"

"No," I told him truthfully. He was just being honest and

sweet. I was the one who was in the wrong.

"Did I do something?"

"No," I said again.

"Then what is it? Because I thought this was all going really well. And now I don't know what happened," Tanner said, clearly trying to keep his voice low and calm. He was failing a little.

"It's just..." How could I tell him that even though I had felt something a few moments ago, I had Ryker?

"Oh." Clarification was evident in his eyes. "There's someone else."

I did not say anything. To deny it would be to deny Ryker and the feelings I had for him. There was no denying that. But to confirm was to give away Ryker, and possibly the secret that we shared about who I really was.

Unfortunately, I think my silence was the confirmation he needed.

Tanner kicked his iPod away from where we were standing by several feet, narrowly missing the edge of the pond.

"Why would you even agree to a date with me if you were seeing someone else?" He spun on me and shouted.

I flinched. I had never seen Tanner angry before. It was not something I ever cared to see again.

"I don't know what to say," I whispered. "You were so persistent, and I didn't want to hurt you."

He cowered over me, and I was suddenly aware of just how small I was, and just how big he was.

He backed off and looked at me, shaking his head back and forth.

"You don't have to be scared of me, Maddie." He let out a breath I did not know he was holding. "I'd never hurt you. I'm sorry for losing my temper there."

He walked back to me, slowly and carefully, he wrapped me in his arms and pulled me into him in a hug.

"I'm sorry," he repeated, much calmer.

"I'm sorry, too." I was terribly sorry for leading him on. I never wanted to hurt him or make him feel like he was a pity date. That was the main reason I had said no in the first place. I saw no future with him.

Tanner pulled back just enough to look down at me.

"I guess this just means I have some competition. Good thing I'm the competitive type." He chuckled.

I knew he was joking, but his words still settled weird in my stomach.

"I'll just have to keep sweeping you off your feet until you choose me."

Before I could think about how to respond, he tipped me back and held me suspended in the air halfway to the ground. I did not know he was so strong and well balanced.

His lips crushed into mine.

Involuntarily, my mouth parted slightly for him.

He did not waste a moment.

His tongue invaded my mouth and an explosion of desire sliced through me.

There was no reason I should feel like this while kissing someone that was not my soul mate.

The kiss ended and I was left with the drowsy feeling of wanting more.

"Did you like that, beautiful girl?" he whispered against my lips.

His words sent a shiver down my whole body.

I did not think I could speak even if I wanted to. Which was probably a good thing because in the next breath his lips were on mine again, this time it was begging, intense and erotic.

There was not a cell in my body that did not feel the intensity of his lips on mine.

I wanted more. More kissing, more of him.

I vaguely felt him roaming his hands over my body. There was no skin on skin, but there might as well have been for how it made my flesh burn.

Tanner stopped, mid kiss. His head snapped up and I could see the bottom of his chin as he scanned his head back and forth.

"What is it?" I asked him as I struggled to get into an upright position.

I finally managed to get my own feet under me and stood up to join him in his search of whatever it was he was trying to find.

"Nothing," he said after a few awkward minutes. "I just felt like someone was watching. I thought I heard a noise."

I looked in the general direction he was looking, trying to see if there was any sign of anyone being there.

There was not.

My only thought was of Ryker. How would he feel if he knew I had just been kissing Tanner? More than that, how would he feel if he knew just how much I had been enjoying it?

But he was not there, nobody was.

"It's fine," Tanner said as he turned back to me and grabbed me again, obviously going in for another kiss.

I cannot lie, a large part of me wanted to let him. But the moral and sane part of me told me it was not a good idea.

It was a struggle, but I decided to listen to the latter.

"I can't, really." I placed a hand on his chest to stop him from leaning in any closer.

"You can't deny that chemistry, Maddie," he protested.

"No," I said truthfully. "I can't. But I also can't deny how guilty kissing you makes me feel when there is someone else."

He relented in his attempt to kiss me, backed up a foot away from me and shrugged.

"At least you can admit that there is definitely something between us. Can you at least promise me that you aren't kicking me out of the running until you know exactly what it is?"

Again, I was put in a tough situation. All of me wanted Ryker. I knew without a doubt that I had managed to fall for him in such a short amount of time. There was no mistaking the way I felt about him.

However, I could not deny the feelings that kissing Tanner had evoked in me.

"I promise I will figure out how I feel." That was as close to his request as I would allow myself to go.

I did not want to lead him on any more than I already had, but I also did not want to ignore the remarkable kisses we shared.

"That's good enough for me," he agreed. "Can I walk you to your dorm?"

I looked around us, still on edge after he thought he heard someone.

I was surprised to realize the sun was completely gone, and beyond the circle of light cast by the pond from the lights Tanner had strung up, it was completely pitch black out.

I was in no mood to try to trek across campus in the complete dark.

"Please," I answered him.

His smile was response enough.

Tanner reached for my hand, and I allowed my fingers to intertwine with his. I could feel the weight of the charm bracelet as it dangled elegantly on my wrist. It was a good feeling and only added to the feeling of being graceful and beautiful.

Tanner led me, hand in hand, all the way to my dorm without saying a single word.

He walked me straight up to my dorm room door, kissed me lightly on the cheek, and with a whispered 'goodnight' walked away, smiling as he went.

What had I gotten myself into?

I spun around and walked through my dorm to see Ally sitting on the couch, smiling smugly, holding a cup of tea.

"How was your date?" she asked politely.

"It wasn't a date," I lied. "It was—"

"I know, I know. It was a 'study session'." She used her fingers to air quote the last two words and enunciated them dramatically. "But nobody goes to a study session dressed like that. And your cheeks are flushed, and your lips are swollen. And... oh my goodness!" Ally jumped up and flew across the room to me. "He finally gave you the charm bracelet?"

She had jerked my hand up and was studying the bracelet closely.

"Okay," I finally admitted even though I did not need to since she already knew. "It was a date."

"No duh!" She threw my hand down. "And by the looks of your lips, it ended pretty nicely. So, spill. I want every detail."

"There really isn't much to tell. He made me grilled cheese, we danced, and he kissed me. That's it."

She looked skeptical, but I could see she would accept that answer. For now, at least.

"Are you going to see him again?" Ally asked me.

"I don't think so." I honestly was not sure. I wanted there to be Ryker, and only Ryker. Adding Tanner to the mix had made it all take a confusing turn, and I really did not want any more things to be confusing in my life.

Besides, I needed to think about this practically.

If I was able to get my memories back, I would be able to turn myself back into a fairy. Where would Tanner even be able to fit in? I had no idea if fairies and humans had relations, but I doubted it.

When I was turned back into a fairy, would I even want relations with a human? Probably not.

It was probably for the best to just end it with Tanner.

"Ally," I spoke out loud without realizing it.

"What's up?"

It was now or never. I had to believe that my best friend would help me through it.

"I'm a fairy."

She blankly stared at me, as if she was not sure how to process the information.

"You're a what?" she finally asked.

"A fairy. Well, a fairy queen." I corrected myself.

I figured she would tell me I was insane, or at the very least ask a million and one questions in the very Ally-like way she had.

She did neither.

Instead, she tossed her head back so far that her hair reached her waist, and she cackled.

I waited for her to finish.

It took a few minutes.

When she caught her breath again and was able to stop hysterically laughing, she wiped a tear from her eye and sighed.

"Maddie, why would you say that you're a fairy?" She glanced down at my wrist. "Because of that?"

"No." I self-consciously put my hands behind my back to get the bracelet out of view. I never should have accepted it from Tanner. "You've missed a lot."

I was having a hard time trying to figure out where to begin. Part of me felt like I should be as detailed as I could, but it also seemed like this was a less is more kind of situation.

"You don't really think you're a fairy, do you?" Ally interrupted my thoughts.

She was definitely not making this any easier.

Ally was the one person I needed to understand, that I needed to have on my side.

"No," I said carefully. "I know it."

She scoffed at me, which only resulted in hurting my feelings.

"Why would you 'know' you're a fairy? A fairy queen at that!" She was practically shouting.

I could only imagine what the students in our neighboring dorm rooms were thinking.

All they could probably hear was someone yelling about being a fairy.

"It's hard to explain…" I knew I was beating around the bush. I knew I needed to just be open with her. But the truth was, I was terrified of the truth still. And her reaction so far was not giving me much hope that she was going to be as understanding as I thought she was going to be.

"Well try," Ally demanded and crossed her arms in front of her chest. She looked mad at me. "Because so far you aren't doing that great of a job."

"I met someone while you were gone." I chose my words carefully. I did not want to give away too much information until I knew how she was going to handle it, and my guess was she was not going to handle it well at all. "He knew me in my other life, he's been helping me figure out who and what I am."

"What are you talking about?" Ally put her arms on my

shoulders and shook me like I had some screws loose and shaking me would magically tighten them back into place. "Tanner told me you had been acting weird all weekend. What's really going on?"

"What?" I had only seen Tanner for a few hours over the weekend, not nearly enough for him to think I was acting weird. And if anything, him coming out with all of these feelings for me was making me believe he was acting out of character. "What did he say?"

"He told me how you had been babbling in your sleep, but he couldn't make out exactly what you were saying. He said he came over for a movie night, and then you kicked him out. He came back a little later to check on you and you had passed out; he stayed all night to make sure you were okay."

"I was asleep?" No, I could not have been asleep that whole time, there was no way I could have made all of that up in a dream.

I battled so hard to finally believe in what Ryker was telling me; I fought everything in my mind telling me that it was all a crazy daydream, or that he was a figment of my imagination.

Was that why I could kiss Tanner so passionately? Because Ryker was not real at all, and I only made him up?

But everything in my land was so real. I knew the sounds and the smells; I knew my people from so far below me. I knew the bed chambers. I had felt in my bones and finally believed that there actually was more to my life than what I had thought there was. I believed that I really was someone; that I truly mattered and was important.

Was all of it a lie?

My knees began to shake, and I was afraid I would no longer be able to hold myself up.

Ally, being the dutiful best friend she had always been, must have figured that out and helped me to the couch so that I could sit down.

"Maddie, Tanner said that you were zonked out almost all weekend. What happened?" Ally sat down carefully next to me, keeping one arm around me in support and love.

"I honestly have no idea, but I want to talk to him."

"Who?" she asked me. I could see that she was gravely concerned. Her perfectly symmetrical eyebrows were pinched together, and the corners of her mouth were turned down.

Something was seriously wrong.

"Tanner. I need to talk to him. I need to see what happened, what I said while I was asleep."

"Oh, hunny." The pity in her voice aggravated me. I was not some small, injured child. I was a grown woman. I just had some questions that I thought only Tanner could answer, since he said he was there the whole time. "I don't think that's such a good idea. He likes you, and you guys could really have something together one day. Don't bother him with this stuff. He's worried about you, don't make it any worse."

"What are you trying to say, Ally?" I knew I had allowed myself to go monotone and sound cold, but I did not care. The things she was insinuating hurt, annoyed, and angered me.

"I'm just saying that not every guy likes crazy. I think you're having some trouble keeping dream and reality separate. I want to help you, but I can't if you don't let me."

So, Ally really did think I was crazy after all.

Truthfully, I was starting to join her in that conclusion.

Still, I did not like the way her thought process was going and preferred for her to change it entirely.

"Ally," I spoke calmly and carefully, taking extreme care

with the words I chose. "Why do you think I had the dreams that I had?"

"It could be a lot of things," she said sadly. "You could just be stressed, or maybe you got heat stroke. It was a really hot weekend. I know you haven't been sleeping well, maybe it was because you were overly exhausted, and sleep deprived. Maybe it was a combination of any of those. In any case, I want you to know that it was all just a dream."

I nodded, not knowing what to say, or trusting myself to speak even if I did have the words.

It seemed like I had another major decision to try and figure out.

I was not ready to give up being a fairy queen. I knew nothing of what it entailed, and, for all I knew, I hated being a queen. But as of now, with no memory of my prior self, I knew I wanted to rule my race. I knew that I wanted the love and respect and power that came along with the title.

I could, however, go without the constant battling, the not being able to actually be with my soul mate, and the part about having multiple lovers.

But I wanted everything else. My mission now, as long as I knew that was what I wanted, was to make everyone else believe that I was normal and just pulling an elaborate ruse on them.

"You must be right." I plastered on my most relieved look. "I had to have just been overly tired. A fairy queen? What was I thinking?"

Ally smiled brightly, all traces of concern and worry completely erased.

I was extremely glad that she bought it because I was under way too much stress to try to figure out another way of convincing her that I was okay.

"Good," she said cheerily. "Then let's go to bed. I am so tired from the weekend, and we have class bright and early!"

Ally clapped her hands chipperly and sprung up from her seat. She practically skipped to the bedroom door.

I followed her in the most normal 'me' way that I could think of. It dawned on me how strange and ironic it was to try to be myself. I had been me for over two decades, and here I was trying to be me.

I followed her into the bedroom, did not bother changing, and climbed into bed.

Ally passed out quickly, her heavy breathing turning into light snores after only ten minutes or so.

It took me much longer to fall asleep.

Every time I would even get close to drifting off, I swore I heard my name being whispered.

Each time, I would fling up in my bed, squint my eyes in the dark and scan the room.

Each time I saw the same thing. Ally and I were the only ones in there, and nobody was saying my name.

And then it would take me a very long time until I was close to drifting off again.

There was just far too much going through my mind.

To summarize it all – I was a twenty-two-year-old orphaned girl, who was actually a fairy queen disguised as an orphaned girl. I had met my soul mate, though for whatever reasons that still baffled me, I could not be with him. I had a whole race of fairies to save, and I could only do that by gaining my memories and returning myself back into a fairy. If I failed in doing that, my whole race would be killed. If I was successful, then I had to fight off a fairy king of another court that wanted to marry me and kill me for my powers.

The icing on the cake was, I was completely alone, and had to pretend to even my best friend that I was perfectly normal and that there was nothing strange going on in my head.

I eventually passed out, ignoring my name being whispered frantically over and over. I slept the rest of the night, fitfully and restlessly.

CHAPTER 7

I woke up the next morning feeling stiff and even more tired than when I had gone to bed

"Good morning, sleepyhead!" Ally's chipper voice rang through the residue of my sleepy state.

I sat up, every joint in my body feeling stiff, my mind more tired than I could ever recall it having ever felt.

I had the strange feeling that I had a very important dream, but for the life of me I could not remember a single detail about it. The harder I tried to remember anything, the further away it all seemed.

"You need to get up if you want to get breakfast before class." Ally had her back to me but was watching me carefully through the reflection in the mirror she was at, grooming her glorious hair.

Knowing that she was studying me, I got out of bed as normally as I could, ignoring the way my body screamed at me with every move I made.

"Great." I tried to match her pep. "I'm starving!"

I quickly dressed, making sure to make a big show out of selecting my clothes like I normally would.

I was painfully aware of her eyes following me the entire time, and I could only hope that I appeared perfectly fine.

"Ready?" I smiled at her as I threw my hair up in the bun that it normally ended up in.

She returned the smile, held out her elbow for me to hook

arms, and we walked together to the dining hall.

The moment we entered the main hall, the smell of all the food wafted over me and made me realize just how hungry I really was.

At least I could stop pretending long enough to get some food in my stomach.

Ally and I met back at our normal table at the far end of the hall that was ill lit and rarely occupied by any other students.

"Wow." Ally's eyes widened when she saw my plate.

It was overflowing.

"What?" I asked around a mouthful of bacon. "I had trouble deciding what I wanted."

"I can see that." Ally laughed at me.

I could no longer see any hesitation in her. She looked like she was fully convinced by my acting; I could only hope she really was.

We ate for a while in silence, partly because we were both so busy stuffing forkfuls of food into our mouths, but mostly because I had nothing to say. I was worried that if I said anything, I would blurt out that I was a fairy, again.

I did not need to do that.

"Hey." Tanner swooped into the bench next to Ally. He had his own plate full of food.

I did not even look up at him. I was mortified after last night.

It hit me just how awkward our friendship was going to become, especially after that heated kiss.

I nodded in his general direction as a way of greeting, hoping my mouth full of food was excuse enough for not talking to him.

"You could have given me a heads up about your 'study session'!" Ally smacked his arm, smiling at him.

Tanner cut his eyes to me, obviously trying to confirm with

me if I had spilled the beans or if she was trying to trap him into giving something up that he should not say.

I nodded slightly, trying to convey with the simple movement that I had, indeed, told her about the date.

"We, uh…" He shrugged and gave a soft chuckle. "We didn't want to say anything until we knew if there would be a second date or not."

"Is there?" Ally looked back and forth between the two of us rapidly, impatient for an answer from either of us.

I was about to tell her no, there would not be a second date, and that even though the first one was lovely, I was only interested in being friends.

"Well, you don't share a kiss like we did and not follow up with a second date." Tanner beat me to speaking.

"You told me he kissed you." Ally beamed at me. "But I think you neglected to tell me just how awesome it was. I want all the details." Ally placed her elbows on the table and rested her chin on her folded hands, staring me down like she could intimidate the information out of me.

Sadly, she probably could use that tactic on me effectively.

However, with Tanner sitting right there, staring at me just as intently as Ally was, there was no way I could say anything about the kiss, good or bad.

"I'm not talking about it," I said in response to both of their stares.

"Fine." Ally turned her inquisitional look to Tanner. "You spill."

"It was the most amazing feeling, sparks, fireworks, butterflies. You name it, it was there in that kiss. She can't deny it." He kept his eyes locked on mine, not breaking contact at all, not even long enough to blink.

My heart started to beat faster with the intensity and lust he was showing me so publicly. I was completely mortified, and I knew I was blushing. I could feel the unwanted heat rising from the base of my neck all the way to my hairline.

"Shut. Up." Ally slammed her hand onto the tabletop palms down, making a loud noise and causing the people closest to us to look in our direction.

Tanner was still staring at me intently, and as hard as I tried, I could not look away from him. It was like a magnet was pulling my glance in his direction and I could not pull away even if I wanted to.

"So will there be a second date?" Ally's voice was rising steadily in her excitement. No doubt, she felt like the most skilled match maker ever to grace the earth.

"Will there?" Tanner echoed her question.

I was being put on the spot. I hated being put on the spot. I always felt like a deer in the middle of the road, unsure of which way to go so instead of moving to safety I just stand there, big eyed, and wait until I get seriously injured or die.

"How about Friday night, dinner?" he suggested as if I had confirmed already that I wanted to see him again.

"Yes," Ally spoke for me. "She would love to."

I was even more embarrassed that I could not unfreeze long enough to answer for myself. Which, if I could have, I would have said no.

"I'll make you dinner, meet me at my dorm around seven?"

"It's a date," Ally said and clapped her hands.

"Great." Tanner got up and grabbed his empty plate from the table. "I look forward to having you all to myself again, Maddie." He left me and Ally at the table.

I watched him leave, completely stupefied.

It had not fully registered what had happened.

I was going on a second date with Tanner? In his dorm?

What had I gotten myself into?

Wait, no. More accurately, what had Ally gotten me into?

"You can thank me at the wedding." Ally stuffed a bit of cold egg into her mouth and chewed happily.

"What did you just do?" I whispered.

"You clearly wanted to say yes," she defended herself. "And, anyways, you two obviously have chemistry if your kiss was that good. It was good, wasn't it?"

"That is so not the point!" I could feel my temper rising and I had to really struggle to keep it under control so I would not make a bigger scene than I already had.

"So, you admit it! It was good!"

"It doesn't matter!" I was quickly losing the thin veil of self-control. "You don't speak for me. You don't make decisions for me. I am my own person and am perfectly capable of making up my own mind without someone else doing it for me!"

Okay. The veil tore, and my anger flowed. I had shouted the last part at her, and I knew half the dining hall was now watching.

But I did not care, I might as well give them something to watch.

I snatched my plate off the table, flipped her the bird, and stormed out of the dining hall as fast as I dared go on my clumsy feet.

I could hear the excited buzz of the other students as they began to gossip and speculate about me and what had just happened before the door was even finished closing behind me.

Whatever. Let them talk. Let them jump to whatever conclusions they wanted to jump to. I was way too annoyed and angry to care what anyone else thought about it.

I was rushing so fast from the dining hall I ran smack into someone.

Someone large, someone strong.

Those strong arms held me steady, kept me from falling, and finally wrapped around me and held me close.

I leaned into the hard chest and cried. I cried because I had no idea what was going on in my life, and no idea how to change it or correct it. I cried because I was no longer in control of anything around me and it was all becoming far too overwhelming.

"It's okay, my Queen," Ryker whispered into the top of my head.

"How can it be okay? Nothing is right any more." I sobbed into his shirt. I knew my words were muffled, but I also had the feeling that he would understand me anyways.

"I know it seems that way, but you have me, forever and always."

His words calmed me. His voice soothed me.

My sobs calmed into hiccups and sniffles, my hands that I had not realized were fisted into his t-shirt relaxed, and my breathing steadied out.

"How did you find me?" I picked my head up enough to glance up at him through my wet, mascara clumped eyelashes.

"I could feel you. Your sense of distress and unhappiness were overwhelmingly strong. I know I should stay away, but I needed to make sure you were all right."

So, he could still feel me even when we were not in the same area.

Does that mean he could feel me last night when Tanner kissed me?

Would asking about it condemn me or help me?

"What causes you to feel my emotions?" I had to ask. That was the most innocent and vague way I could think of to ask him how it worked and what exactly it was he felt.

He took his time answering, and I was sure it was because he was battling in his own mind what would be the right thing to say.

"The stronger your emotion, the stronger I feel it," he said slowly. "When your sorrow is intense, I know you are upset. When you feel extreme happiness, I can feel that, too."

I think he just confirmed he felt me last night, without having to say the words. I was an awful person.

"Don't be sorry." He followed my train of thought.

"I don't want anyone else. I want you."

He smiled, but it was a sad smile. There was no happiness in it.

"I want you, too, my Queen. But we can't." He shrugged. "I signed up for this, I knew what I was getting myself into."

"Why can't we turn you into a royal? If you were to become a royal, we could be together," I argued with him.

"It isn't that easy."

"Why not?" I shouted. I wanted just one thing to be easy, one thing to go the way I would like for it to go.

"There are things that need to happen in order for me to become a royal, sacrifices I would have to make. I am not willing to do that."

"Not even for me, for love?" I pushed out of his arms and stood a foot away from him.

It genuinely hurt me to know that there could be a loophole that allowed us to be together and he was not willing to take it. "What would you have to sacrifice?"

"I really don't think we should be talking about this right

now." He looked around to make sure everyone was out of earshot. "I think I have a lead on getting your memories back."

All thoughts of love and betrayal and anger vanished. It took me a second for his words to register, to understand their meaning.

"What, how?"

"I need to look more into it, but just know that I am working tirelessly to help you, to bring you back to me. I need to go now that I know you're okay. Can we meet at the end of the week? I think I will need some time to dig a little deeper into my theory, but I want to restore your memories as soon as possible."

"Of course." I was in shock that the conversation had taken the turn it had.

If there was a chance that he could be restoring my memories so soon, I wanted to jump on it, and quickly.

"I will see you soon." He kissed my forehead briefly and was gone.

I really wanted to learn how he did that.

Though, if I got my memories back, I suspected I already would know how to do it.

With more joy in my step, and more hope in my heart, I jogged off to my first class of what could possibly end up as my last week as a human college student.

CHAPTER 8

The week moved slowly, I felt like I was on autopilot for the whole thing.

After such a crazy weekend, I figured the week would be just as crazy, if not more.

But it was not.

The most exciting part was, how I envisioned it to be, playing the most intense game of hide and seek ever played.

Any time I saw Tanner, I ducked and hid however I could.

Sometimes that meant I was crouching behind a garbage can, hiding behind my books, or closely following a random group of students making their way across campus.

At one point, someone turned around and asked me if they could help me. Something in their tone suggested they were not actually offering help of any kind.

Ally had asked me midway through the week why I was avoiding Tanner, to which I had to lie and say that I was not avoiding him, just very busy.

She informed me that he had witnessed me earlier that day ducking around a bush when I saw him.

I lied, again, and told her that I had dropped my pencil and was only looking for it.

I could tell she did not believe me. But, oh well. I had bigger problems.

The week had come and gone, and here I was, Friday at lunch, with the clock dwindling down to this impending date that

I did not want to go on.

I was hoping, since he obviously knew I was avoiding him, that he would come to his senses and just cancel the date. But I felt like I would not be able to get that lucky.

My life was not exactly the easy life any more.

Instead of going to any classes today and risking seeing Tanner, I hid out in my dorm. Ally did not even know I skipped classes today. The only class we shared on Fridays was the dreaded philosophy course that slept through way more than I should have. And if she asked, I could just tell her that I got caught up in a study session for another class and lost track of time. I would tell her that when I finally realized how late it was, I opted to skip that class. The professor already hated me; she would believe me when I told her that I would rather not go in late.

Still, laying on the dorm room couch, doing nothing but staring at the ceiling, made the day tick by agonizingly slow.

I was ready to get up, go outside and get some fresh air.

Or at the very least, some food, I was reminded by my grumbling stomach.

But the risk of seeing Tanner was too high, and even though it was impossible, I was hoping the old cliché 'out of sight, out of mind' would apply here.

Wishful thinking.

Tanner had been blowing up my phone all week, and today it had already gone off over a dozen times. I refused to acknowledge any messages from him today.

Earlier in the week I had replied to him a handful of times, only to try to tip him off the trail of me avoiding him.

Wishful thinking, again.

As if thinking about it made it happen, my phone buzzed.

I glanced at the screen before it dimmed. Sure enough, Tanner was texting me again.

I will have my roommate gone before you get here. Everything will be ready for seven.

Well, so much for that theory.

I could just text him back and tell him that I thought I had a stomach bug. I had skipped all my classes today, so it could be believable.

But then he might want to bring the date over here, and then what would even be the point?

Even if he did bring it here, I could not count on Ally to stay here so we would not be alone. She was rooting for us to get married, for crying out loud. The second he got here she would leave with some phony excuse as to why she had to go.

I could just tell him that he did not have to send his roommate away.

It was not exactly like he bothered me so much, it was just a little creepy how he sat there and stared without saying a word.

But I could happily deal with that if the alternative was an evening alone with Tanner in his dorm.

His roommate, Frankie, could be the thing that keeps Tanner from becoming physical, and then I would not have to put off the date and hurt anyone. It seemed like the most logical plan. And, since it was the only plan I had, that was what I was going to go with.

You don't have to kick Frankie out, will feel bad for him if you make him leave. Please let him stay. Seven still works.

There. I sent the text, satisfied with my decision to include Frankie in the date.

Not that there was anything particularly satisfying about going on a second date with someone that you did not even want to go on a first date with.

But at least after tonight I could tell him that I was truly not interested, and let it be in the past.

Hopefully, after tonight, Ryker would figure out how to restore my memories so I would not have to worry about Tanner at all.

But we would cross that bridge when we got there.

My stomach grumbled again, loudly.

Now that I no longer had to avoid Tanner, I supposed it would be all right to risk running into him to grab some food.

I was tired of the dining hall, and I really did not want to eat at a booth alone. So, I grabbed my wallet and keys, and figured I would venture off campus to the local McDonalds and just get something cheap to munch on. I did not mind sitting there alone. I could grab a book and sit there for a while, away from campus and away from the mess of my life.

McDonalds was not far to drive; it was only about ten minutes off campus. It was nice, though, because most of the students on campus did not really go out and dine at other places since there were a few restaurants and the main dining hall available any time.

I barely ever even left campus to eat.

It was a treat to myself to get away, and I desperately needed a treat right now.

I pulled up in the parking lot, found a spot right away and parked.

It was another really nice day, and it made me feel a little silly for hiding inside all day long. I could have spent my entire day in a much smarter way. There were some water parks nearby, a zoo, even the mall would have been more fun than sitting in my dorm room, closed in, and avoiding everyone.

But it was too late now. I could at least take advantage of the next few hours and enjoy some time out and about.

I glanced in the rearview mirror before I got out to check the mascara that I hastily applied before I left. Since that was the only makeup I ever really bothered to wear, I at least wanted it to look nice.

I checked the mirror one last time as I reached for the door of the car and froze, fingers wrapped around the handle.

My eyes had to be playing tricks on me.

There was no possible way I was actually seeing what I thought I was seeing.

Tanner and Ally were in the McDonalds window, sitting together at a table enjoying their meals.

What were they doing?

Why was I feeling so uneasy, watching them eat and laugh together?

They probably hung out all the time, a lot more than I knew about. After all, Tanner had told me that Ally knew about his crush. That alone indicated that they spent time together without me at least once in a while.

Maybe they were just going over details for the date? It was possible he was just running ideas by her. He said that she helped him pick out the bracelet, so it made sense that he ran a lot by her where I was concerned.

I could justify that. She was my best friend and knew me better than anyone else, he was a smart guy, and he knew that she would have all the answers.

Still, it did not settle right, seeing the two of them at the table together.

Now I was left with the dilemma of leaving and pretending I had not seen them or going in and just joining their lunch.

I squinted harder, trying to see their trays to better gauge how long they had been there and if it would even be worth me going in.

What was Ally holding?

It did not look like they had much food left at all, but it did look like they were studying something. They both had their heads bowed down low, and they were occasionally lifting their heads to say something to each other.

I briefly wondered if they had a test coming up and that was why they had met up without me. That would have explained a lot, too.

But I know Ally's schedule. She had no tests coming up at all. She had just finished all of her midterms, so she would not have any tests for quite a while.

So that theory did not hold up.

They were both obviously reading something intently, and I really wanted to know what it was.

I did not think it would be wise to go in and join them, though. So, I decided to stay put, my grumbling stomach completely forgotten.

I was so distracted with watching them, I did not see Ryker walking up to, or materializing by, my car.

His quick knock on my window made me jump a foot out of my seat.

I held a hand to my chest and closed my eyes with my head leaned back while I took a moment to catch my breath before opening the window to see what he wanted.

With my pounding heart slowed down, I opened my eyes back up to talk to Ryker, but he had vanished.

"Where did he go?" I mumbled to myself, trying to see where he had gone off to.

"Right next to you." He was in the passenger seat.

Again, I jumped.

All of this was going to give me a heart attack; I was going to just keel over dead any minute from all of the constant scares.

"Sorry." Ryker placed a hand on my shoulder.

His touch rapidly calmed my racing heart, and I was able to breathe again.

"What are you doing?" I asked him, still not sure why he had to be so dramatic with his entrances all the time. "Did you figure it out, how to restore my memories?"

"Well, first, I missed you too." He laughed.

Oops, I suppose it had been almost a week since I had seen him. It was kind of a weird thought to realize that I did not really miss him as much as I imagined I would miss my soul mate after almost a week.

Maybe it was because I had already spent over a century with the man, and in my bones, I knew that I would have a few more centuries, so what were a few days, really?

It sounded good to me.

"I missed you, too." I smiled at him.

"But, to answer your question, yes. I think I have figured it out. Before I tell you, though, you need to promise me pardon on my crimes if you are able to gain your memories."

"Pardon for your crimes?" I repeated. What did he have to do to get this information? "What kind of crimes are we talking here?"

"First, promise me pardon."

"Fine, I won't hold anything you did against you for returning my memories," I assured him.

"Good." He took a deep breath before he continued. "I had to go into your private laboratory."

I had to laugh. He just told me I had a private laboratory, what on earth would I need a laboratory for?

"I'm serious," he shot at me. "It is a serious crime, one penalized with death, to enter your private laboratory without your explicit consent. If anyone knew I was in there, I would not be alive right now to tell you what I learned."

"Why is it so bad to go into a room? And why do I even need a lab?" I could not help but let a few more chuckles out as I asked the insane questions.

"It's your law, your lab. After researching and pilfering through everything, I can see why you made it a law." He shivered as if he was mortified by some of the memories from his week in my lab.

"What was in there?" I was genuinely curious to know what was so horrible that I made a whole law about keeping people out, with such horrific repercussions and would make such a huge, strong warrior tremor in fear.

"That isn't what's important." He looked back at me; his eyes shone bright with excitement. "I know how to get your memories back, at least I think I do. It's the best shot we have, and we really don't have much time left to try to come up with other things."

"Great, what do I have to do? Do I need to drink some type of potion? Say a prayer? I am willing to do anything."

"I'm glad you said that." He drew back, somehow making his giant frame shrink. "Because what you have to do is going to be very, very hard."

"What could be that bad? I need to save my people; wouldn't anything be worth that?"

"You have to die, my Queen."

"Die?" I whispered. "How would restoring my memories be

useful if I'm dead?"

"That's the thing. All of my research suggests that if you die, only the human part will die. The fairy queen part, which is royal and nearly immortal, will live on. The human will be washed away, leaving only your prior self."

"And what if that doesn't work?" I shouted at him. I was furious that in all this time, he was suggesting that I just up and die. "Then I will just be dead, and my people will continue to perish. Is that really a better alternative than what we have going on now?"

"I have a theory." He tried to defend himself.

"Oh, he has a theory." I was hysterical. Being told that I had to go die on top of everything else was a little too much for me to deal with.

"Please, hear me out, my Queen."

Ryker placed a hand on my knee, calming me down as much as I suspected I could be calmed down at the moment.

"Okay, I'm listening."

"I also have a wonderful ability to heal people, it is another reason why I have been such a useful protector to you all these years. As the human in you dies, I would know if it's working, because I would feel my queen more and more. Feeling you would grow stronger. But if it doesn't, if it grows dimmer, I could stop, and heal you. We would know then that my research was wrong, and that I need to get back to your lab. If it works, then we restore your memories and previous genetic makeup and you become the powerful queen that we need to save our people."

His plan sounded, in theory, like it would work.

"What if you can't feel me, but you are unsuccessful in healing me?" The risk was obvious to me. I was sort of surprised it was not as obvious to him.

"I have contemplated that scenario." He moved his gaze to look out the front windshield. I had the distinct impression that he was avoiding looking at me. "But there is no solution for that. I don't know the outcome of how this would go for sure, but I know it is the closest I have come to any type of answer, and I know we need to do something."

I could not believe this was the answer that we were looking for. I refused to accept that this was the only solution and there was no other way to restore my memories.

It all seemed way too risky, way too intense and way too real.

And I was way too unprepared for all of it.

"I know this seems like a lot, but you have my reassurance that I will not let anything happen to you." He turned to face me, grabbing me to force me to face him. "I love you, Maddie. I always have, and I always will. I will make sure you come out of this alive, either as you are now or as my queen. I will not lose you again."

I believed him. As much as I did not want to go through with all of this, I trusted that he would make sure I remained safe, no matter what the cost.

"What's your plan?"

"My plan is going to sound a little morbid."

"What is it?"

"I would like to cut you, I have an acute sense of the living and the dead, I believe I have a way of causing just enough injury to send you into an 'in between' state, allowing me to see if I can sense you more without actually fully killing you."

"You want to cut me?"

"I don't want to," he corrected me. "I believe that by cutting you, I will be allowing your human self to slip just enough to glimpse if the queen is underneath. But not so much so that I would not be able to easily bring you back and heal you completely if I needed to."

"I need time to think about this, I don't know what to do or how to respond to anything that you're suggesting."

"I understand that." He sighed a long, impatient sigh. "But you need to keep aware of how low our numbers are dwindling. Our race is going to die out and we won't be able to do anything about it."

I thought of my people in the street far below my bed chambers, of the little children playing in the streets. Were they still alive? Or was this king so horrible that he would kill innocent children just to get me to come out of hiding?

The gorgeous woman holding her infant in the pool, would that baby be left motherless because I hesitated in doing what I needed to do in order to retain my memories?

I could not have that on my shoulders. I could not stand to see any of my people hurt, grieving the loss of their loved ones while blindly following me even in my absence, just waiting for me to show up and save the day.

Those thoughts weighed heavy on my heart; tears threatened to betray the emotions I worked to conceal.

"I just need a little bit of time." I barely choked back.

Ryker nodded but said nothing more on the topic.

"Are you going out with him again?" Ryker had followed my gaze in the rearview mirror and had easily spotted Ally and Tanner.

I had not even noticed that I was watching them again.

"Yes."

He remained silent. He was either watching them with me or watching me as I watched them. I was not sure which, but I did not care.

The safer, simpler topic of trying to decipher what they were studying was the only thing I wanted to concentrate on for the time being.

Eventually, I felt the absence of his presence, and I knew without even looking over at the passenger seat that he had disappeared.

Ally and Tanner were still engrossed in their studies, and I had completely lost my appetite. Something about being told I had to be cut up to near death did something to the stomach that food would probably not sit well with.

Instead of going in to eat like I had originally intended, I started my car back up and left the parking lot feeling alone, desperate, and full of more despair than I cared to admit to anyone.

I crossed over onto campus, pulled up outside my dorm building, and cried in my car for several minutes.

How had I gotten in so over my head? I felt like I was being continually punched in the gut, and someone was wringing my heart out repeatedly. My head was pounding from a tension migraine, and I knew no matter what I did I would not be able to get rid of it. I was miserable through and through.

I trudged up to my dorm, closed the door behind me, made my way into the bathroom, stripping as I went, turned on the hot water of the shower and climbed in.

I had absolutely no intention of showering. I only wanted the steam of the scalding water to loosen up any of the tight knots covering my entire body. I felt like I had just run a few marathons back-to-back with no rest, no food, and no water.

I sat on the floor of the tub, wishing the water could also wash away the last week.

But I knew it could not.

I needed a vacation. I needed to get away.

"Maddie!" Ally's voice cut through my private time. "Maddie, where are you?"

"I'm in the bathroom!" I opted to not tell her anything about my trip to McDonalds.

I was positive their lunch was innocent. Even if I were to believe Ryker about Tanner being dangerous, I knew Ally. She would never hurt me, ever.

She walked right into the room and pulled the curtain aside.

"What are you doing?" I asked her, scrambling to cover myself up.

"Where were you today?" Ally demanded.

I snatched the curtain from her hands so I could stand up and use it to cover myself so that I could talk to her.

I had completely forgotten the excuse I was going to tell her to get me out of missing philosophy class.

"I, uh, I just didn't feel like going," I said. "I have a migraine."

"You didn't miss much. Class was pretty boring; I almost fell asleep."

"That's great." I rolled my yes at her. "Can I get back to my shower now?"

"Oh, sorry. Don't forget about your big date!" Ally sang as she left the bathroom and closed the door behind her.

I did not even know what time it was. I really did not care. With how long I was sitting at McDonalds watching them and talking to Ryker, it was easily four or five in the evening.

Sighing, I took my shower, blow dried my massive hair, applied my mascara, and grabbed whatever clothes I reached first.

I truly did not care what I wore. I had no intention of going any further with Tanner anyways. And I would be dying soon, so who cared what I looked like for a date that did not matter?

I left my hair down; my migraine had simmered down to a dull thudding. I was in no mood to put more pressure on the top of my head than I needed to.

The clothes I ended up grabbing were a pair of blue jeans covered in frays and a pale, powder blue shirt that was well worn and well loved.

I was not dressing up. I wanted to be comfy. The attire was cozy and satisfying.

"Is that what you're wearing?" Ally burst into the room.

"Yeah."

"How are you supposed to fall in love if you are already ending the effort? You can do better than that."

"I don't want to." She was missing the whole point. I was not the one who agreed to this date, she was. As far as I was concerned, she should be the one dressing up and going to Tanner's dorm for dinner, not me.

She rolled her eyes at me and scoffed in the way only Ally could while still looking impeccable.

"You could at least dress up those jeans with a nicer top. Those jeans could be super sexy if you dress them right."

"I don't want to be sexy. I don't even want to go on this date."

She ignored me; her head buried deep inside the closet. I could hear her murmuring to herself as she made some selections and dismissed them.

"Throw this on." She tossed some clothes at me. "Let me check your jewelry box for some accessories."

"Why are you pushing me so hard on this?" I had really started to feel like I had no choices left in my life. I was not even allowed to decide what to wear on a date I was not allowed to decide to go on.

"Just humor me, please?" Ally handed me some earrings and a necklace. "I promise, if it doesn't go well tonight, I won't push you any more. But he really likes you. At least give him a fair shake."

"Fine." I took off my shirt and pulled on the clothes she had pulled out for me and threw on the jewelry.

Taking another look in the mirror, I had to admit that I looked really good. Ally had a great fashion sense. Not that mine was bad, but I did not put as much thought into my day-to-day outfits as she did. It was rare that I did more than make sure I matched.

She had grabbed me a plain lavender tank top, with a sleeveless, black, short, cropped vest that buttoned once just below my chest.

The jewelry I accessorized with was simple, just a long dainty chain that had several golden hoops woven into the chain itself, and earrings that dangled to match.

"One more thing." Ally walked up to me.

She grabbed my hand and clasped the charm bracelet Tanner gave me firmly in place.

"I think it would be nice to wear it on your date." She shrugged. "At the very least, it's a nice gesture, especially if you're going to be letting him down tonight."

She was probably right. Maybe I could even offer to give him the bracelet back. I doubted I would need any jewelry if I died.

"Okay, you're good to go. Maddie, you look stunning."

"Thank you." I glanced at the wall clock, startled to see that it was already after six. "I guess I better get going."

"Go get 'em." She laughed. "I can't wait to hear all about it when you get back tonight."

I walked out without saying anything else. I was worried I would never see her again, and I hated goodbyes.

But really, what was I worrying about? I had no idea when Ryker would show back up, and even when he did show up, I did not know when this horrific ordeal was going to take place. I was as in the dark as anyone else.

I took my time walking, trying to plan out exactly what I would say to Tanner, how I could let him down firmly so that he would know I meant it, without tarnishing his overall opinion of me.

I knew I would probably never see him again, but our friendship still mattered, and I did not want anything to ruin it.

It was a nice evening, so the walk, at least, was enjoyable. The sun was bright, barely starting to sink yet. Birds were chirping happily, oblivious to the turmoil running through my mind and heart. Even all the students I passed seemed extra happy.

On a regular weekend, I would have looked like any of them, excited for the weekend to relax and enjoy the outdoors with no classes or alarm clocks.

But I felt like there was a storm cloud brewing over my head. Like those commercials on antidepressants, where the woman walks through a happy crowd, while she is miserable with a massive dark cloud hanging above her, and she is holding a picture of herself smiling in front of her face. I felt like her.

I passed a few people I knew, they gave me cheery hellos, and I felt like such a fraud returning the sentiment.

Tanner's dorm was halfway across campus, and I managed to make it take over twenty minutes to make the journey.

It was twenty minutes too fast before I was staring at his

door, debating not even knocking and turning around and never coming back.

The door opened before I had even lifted my fist to make the first knock.

It was Tanner's roommate, Frankie.

"Hey, is Tanner here?"

Frankie stared at me for a moment, I had the weird feeling that he was staring through me and not really noticing me at all.

After a really long, awkward time, Frankie just simply turned around and walked back into the room, leaving the door open for me to enter.

That still left my question of if Tanner was there unanswered. But I took the open door as an invitation to come inside. I did not want to be rude, and there was no point in standing outside in the hallway looking into an open dorm room.

I followed Frankie to the couch and sat down on the opposite end.

Looking anywhere but in his direction, I took in the room.

His dorm was much bigger than the one Ally and I shared. He had his own room, and Frankie had his. Their living room looked more like a whole entertainment center, with every gaming system imaginable lined neatly on shelves, surrounding a massive TV mounted on their wall.

I knew from prior visits that their bathroom had a jacuzzi tub and a very expensive showerhead that was supposed to massage your scalp as it poured the water down.

I knew that their kitchen had a double oven, dishwasher, and a massive fridge.

They were the rich ones on campus.

From the kitchen, I heard a loud clatter, and I really hoped it was Tanner in there.

Without looking at him, I knew that Frankie was staring at me. I could feel his eyes boring into the side of my skull, like little needles trying to pick my mind apart.

Right before I was about to get up and apologize to Frankie for having to run, Tanner emerged through the kitchen doors carrying a giant silver tray lined with several dishes of steaming food.

"Ah, you're here," Tanner said. He looked at Frankie. "You were supposed to come get me when she arrived. Were you waiting long?" he said back to me.

"Not at all." Anxious to get off the couch, I jumped up to help Tanner with the tray.

"No, no, no." He moved fluidly away from me. You're my date, I am the host. I can't have you helping me." He set the tray down on the dining room table that I never noticed before in the far back end of their massive living space.

"Is this table new?" It was gorgeous, hardwood, hand carved and stained to perfection.

"No, we just normally have a bunch of clutter on it so you can't really see it." He said as he set all the dishes out and arranged them until he was happy with the setting. "Are you sure you don't mind if Frankie joins us? At the very least, he can probably go eat in his room."

I looked back at the couch where Frankie still sat. He was still following my every move.

I felt bad for him. I had no clue what his issues were, but I knew it could not be easy to be excluded all the time, to have people look at you and judge you before they even knew you.

For the first time, I actually looked at him. He was kind of cute, in a different sort of way. He had rounded cheeks, thick hair that curled just over his ears. He was not unfit, but he was not bulk, either. He looked sad, especially in his eyes, like he was in constant pain, and nobody could understand because he lacked the ability to communicate.

"I'm okay if he joins us." I decided.

Tanner set up the third place setting and motioned for Frankie to come over and join us.

We all sat down, and I took in the smorgasbord of food before me.

Tanner had really outdone himself.

There was a pot roast that looked mouthwatering, with all my favorite vegetables, he even had extra mini potatoes thrown in. Homemade fresh baked French bread, a side salad, and even a bowl of steaming mashed potatoes covered in gooey, melty cheese.

Where did he find the time to cook all of this? I knew for a fact that he had been with Ally up until an hour or so ago. Who cooked all of this food?

"It looks delicious," I said truthfully.

My still-empty stomach growled loudly in agreement, making both Tanner and Frankie smile.

I had trouble deciding which smile bothered me more.

"Well, there is plenty, so eat up!" Tanner started to pile food onto all three plates. "And save room for dessert, I made lemon meringue pie."

My mouth watered even more, so much so that I thought I was going to drool right through my closed lips.

Lemon meringue pie was my absolute favorite dessert.

How did he know what all of my favorites were? Unless Ally had told him. I could see her doing that. She was rooting for us to end up together, she definitely would not be above meddling into it so far as to tell Tanner every single thing I liked so that he could better woo me and sweep me off my feet.

Traitor.

"Maddie." Tanner pulled me from my thoughts. "You look incredible. I have to say, I'm having a hard time keeping my eyes off of you. And I am pleased to see that you wore the bracelet that I gave you."

I stopped mid bite, lowering my fork back onto my plate because that was the hand the bracelet was on and it made me extremely self-conscious to have everyone's attention on it.

Even Frankie had changed his focus from my face to my wrist. The first sign of any emotion other than a smile I had ever seen in him was while he fixated on my sparkling wrist, his eyebrows drew together, and he frowned.

"It really is pretty, thank you," I told him.

"Oh, it was nothing." Tanner took a bite from his plate.

I took that opportunity to take my first bite of food all day.

As good as it looked, it tasted even better. I had no clue how he got the flavors so pronounced, but it was like my tastebuds were in hyper mode from pure delight. The meat was juicy and tender, the vegetables were cooked to perfection. Even the bread was crisp and flaky. It was amazing.

"Ready for dessert?" Tanner asked after I devoured my whole plate.

I was not. I ate way too much, my stomach felt like it was going to explode right out of my jeans.

Tanner walked out of the room and came back in a moment later holding the most delectable pie ever. It was bright and vibrant, and I smelled the lemon before he even reached the table.

"Maddie, would you like a slice?"

"Oh, I know I shouldn't, I am so stuffed."

"Just a small piece?" He wafted the scent towards me.

It made my mouth start to moisten all over again.

"You never know when the next time you'll be able to eat pie will be."

"Huh?" That was an odd thing to say. Ally knew me better than anyone. If she was filling Tanner in on all of my secrets, surely, she would have told him about my pie addiction. I barely went a week without at least one slice of the dessert.

"Come in!" he hollered, staring at me. "She's ready."

Who was ready? Who was he talking to? What did I miss?

"That took long enough." Ally walked into the room.

"Ally?" I was beyond confused.

Why was Ally here on my date?

"Are you sure she's ready?" Ally asked Tanner.

"Yeah, she's ready."

"What is going on?" I asked the two of them. I looked back and forth between Ally and Tanner, trying desperately to make some sort of hasty connection that would allow me to figure out what was happening.

It vaguely dawned on me that Frankie was no longer in the room.

"We are having an intervention," Ally said, as if that would help clarify things.

"An intervention for what?"

She opened up the backpack I did not see her carrying and flung out three notebooks onto the table.

"These." She glanced at Tanner, who was staring at me intently, and then back to me. "Tell me what these are."

I did not want to have this talk in front of Tanner, but if Ally was doing this now, it meant that he likely already knew everything, anyways.

"I told you what they were." I tried to evade the question by being as vague as I could.

"No, not really. You showed me these notebooks, and then later told me you were a fairy," Ally said with a tear in one eye. "I need to know what's going on."

I shifted my focus to Tanner, who had at some point decided to remain glued to the notebooks laying on the table.

"I can't say."

"Can't, or won't?" Tanner said quietly, still staring at the notebooks.

"Maddie, we want to help you. You need it," Ally begged me.

"What do you want me to say?" I was feeling cornered. This whole evening was starting to feel like one giant trap, and I was the dumb prey that fell for it.

"I want you to tell me why your notebooks are filled with all these weird symbols, I want you to tell me why you think you're a fairy."

"Weird symbols?" I snatched up one of the notebooks and opened it to a random page.

Sure enough, it was filled with a bunch of symbols, neatly covering line after line. I had no clue what any of it meant. I picked up another notebook, and it was the same thing. The third, after fanning through all the pages frantically, confirmed that all three notebooks held these unknown graphics.

"These aren't the notebooks I wrote," I protested.

"Yes, they are. I didn't know what to make of them at first. I thought you were just playing some cruel joke on me for leaving you for the weekend. Then you started in on all this stuff about how you're a fairy queen and, Maddie, what am I supposed to think?"

"I don't know, Ally," I said honestly. "What do you think?"

I could see the emotions riding over her. First there was hesitation, then uncertainty, followed by fear, and lastly falling on worry.

"I think you're losing it. I think you need help."

So, she did think I was crazy, after all.

"And what role do you play in all of this?" I turned on Tanner. "Did you even like me at all?"

"Of course, Maddie. I told you I liked you before Ally even came back from her weekend away. I had no idea what was going on until a few hours ago."

"And do you think I am crazy?" I asked him bluntly.

"I think you're confused." He shrugged both shoulders. "I don't think talking to someone will do you any harm."

So that was it, then. They both thought I needed to talk to someone and get help.

If only they knew just how screwed up the situation really was.

"Maddie, if you were a fairy queen, why aren't you ruling your people? Why are you attending college courses?" Ally asked me, clearly trying to reason with me.

Fine. If she wanted to think I was crazy, I might as well let her have the whole story.

"My memories were erased," I told her.

"Okay." I could see that she had started to give up. "Then why don't you go back to your subjects?"

"I can't until I get my memories back and revert to my old genetic makeup," I fired back at her. There was no way I could be making this stuff up on the fly, she had to see that it was a serious thing and hear the truth in my voice.

"Do you hear how insane this all sounds?" Ally asked as a tear slipped silently down one cheek. "Just how did you plan on getting your memories back?"

"Dying." I was done playing these games. "At least, getting in a state that's close enough to dying." I looked at Tanner again, who was still stood motionless, absorbing every word I said. "Any more questions?"

"Have you completely lost it? How would almost dying return memories? Are you really planning on hurting yourself?" Ally was close to hysterics, not that I could blame her. If the roles were reversed I imagined I would be pretty on edge, too.

"I met my soul mate. He can feel me when I am the queen. If the human dies, he will be able to know if the queen will live on or if I am purely human now, He can prevent me from dying fully if he cannot sense the queen."

"Interesting." It was the first word Tanner had said since Ally had begun her questioning. He had grown so quiet that I almost forgot he was even standing there.

I focused on him, and he was staring into the kitchen with his arms crossed over his chest and had a major sour look.

"What is your soul mate's name? What does he look like?" Tanner asked, not looking at me at all.

"What does that matter?" That was not the point of what I had told them. "Your jealousy will just have to wait. I tried telling you that there was someone else in the picture and you wouldn't listen."

Tanner and Ally shared a look that I could not interpret. It was one of those 'inside' looks, and I knew then that I was missing something big.

"Should you tell her, or should I?" Tanner asked Ally.

"You can, I've had enough acting today."

Acting?

"We believe you," Tanner whispered to me.

I felt like he was being sarcastic, but I was honestly too baffled by the sudden change in his tone to think too much into his words.

"Maddie." I focused back on Ally. "I know you're a fairy. I've known it your whole life. Well, your whole human life."

I just stared at her. I could hear her words, but it was as if she was saying them in a different language. They were making no sense; they had no meaning.

"My name is not really Ally." She morphed before my eyes, turning into a much more up close and personal version of my subjects that I had seen from my bed chambers. "I am Sharie, I've been your personal advisor and confidant for nearly your entire reign. When you turned yourself human and hid your memories, you had me follow suit in case anything was to go wrong. I am here to help you now."

"Why." I struggled to keep from screaming at her. "Why would you make me feel like such an idiot for coming to you if you knew who I was the entire time?"

"I needed to know that you actually knew who you were." She shrugged her moss green scaled shoulders.

I got out of my seat and walked closer to her, trying to study every detail that I did not have the chance to study from far above my people.

She still had the same human features and shape to her body and her face. I could make out exactly where her nose, mouth, eyes and ears were. The main difference, other than the obvious one being how she was covered in scales, was that her already large and beautiful eyes had doubled in size and turned completely into a honey shade of brown. There were no whites around the color, and no pupil in the middle. The eye was entirely the honey color, and nothing else.

Even in her fairy form, she was stunningly gorgeous.

"Why help me now?"

I felt like Ryker would have said something to me about Ally being someone I could trust if he knew who she really was. Maybe he did not know.

"I know your people are in danger. Before the change, you had asked me to keep my true identity hidden until it was an emergency, or you figured out who you are."

"But I haven't figured it out!" I shouted at her. "I have no clue who I really am, I don't know who anyone really is." I turned on Tanner. "Are you a fairy, too?"

He nodded once but did not morph into his fairy form.

"I do not have the power to change my looks, unfortunately," he said, as if he could read my thoughts. "I was changed, but not in genetic makeup. I simply had help from some lower caste of fairy to disguise my true form. I am to remain like this until the time is right."

"Is that why you gave me the fairy charm bracelet, you knew?"

"I suspected you knew. I used your reaction to the gift as confirmation," Tanner replied.

"Where do I go from here?" I felt defeated, drained, and exhausted. I felt like I had nowhere to go, and nobody to turn to because nobody was really who I thought they were.

"You can come with us." Tanner held out his hand.

For no reason at all, warning bells rang loudly and clearly in my head.

DANGER!

But Tanner was not dangerous. He and Ally were on my side. I just learned that Ally was not only my best friend as a human, but she was also my advisor, and I was her Queen.

Surely, she would not betray me, and he would not, either.

Still, that one word bounced around my brain on loop, clanking and rattling around rapidly.

I was paralyzed where I stood, staring at Tanner and his outstretched hand, waging a war within myself to trust, or to flee.

"Don't." The one simple word was a pained plea behind me.

I spun around to see who it was that spoke; I had never before heard that voice.

Frankie stood there, less than four feet away from me, his face tomato red from some sort of strain, a line of sweat had started beading over his brows and upper lip.

He was obviously in some type of turmoil.

But he had never spoken before. Up until that moment, I thought he was not capable of speaking.

"Don't," he said again, his voice a coarse rasp from the strain within him.

Tanner dashed past me, slammed into Frankie so hard I thought I would see him go flying backwards.

Instead, they collided with a thunderous boom, ricocheting off each other.

Tanner rebounded faster than I thought capable, and manhandled Frankie back through the kitchen door that I assumed he had emerged from.

"Maddie." Ally diverted my attention. "Come with me."

"No." I could not stop my head from shaking. I could not stop my knees from trembling, or my hands from gripping the top of the table to help hold myself up.

I loved Ally. I trusted Ally with all of my life.

But I did not trust Tanner. I did not trust the way he pummeled into Frankie, the way he forced him from the room. And, by the sounds emerging from the behind the closed kitchen door, I certainly did not trust the way he was beating Frankie up into oblivion.

As long as Ally was pairing up with Tanner, I would not go with her.

"Too bad." She shrugged. "I was hoping it would not have to come to this."

I looked at her, tears burning my eyes and blurring my vision.

There was a sudden rush of people in the room that I did not recognize. They had burst through the front door and started swarming me.

Ally had thrown herself on the floor and Tanner was holding her; they were both crying.

"She's insane!" Ally wailed.

One of the strange men grabbed me and pinned my arms behind my back.

Another man leaned over to help Tanner pick Ally up off the floor, while a third man started firing questions at them.

"What happened?" he asked in a serious, deep baritone.

"She's been acting so strange lately, I thought nothing of it." Ally was back on her feet, leaning heavily on Tanner who had his arms wrapped firmly around her. "But then I found these notebooks." She gestured with her head to where the notebooks full of strange symbols lay. "And then I saw what she did to our friend. When I confronted her, she attacked me, screaming a bunch of nonsense."

"That's not true," I argued.

"Ma'am," the man asking the questions directed at me. "What are these notebooks?"

Another man emerged through the kitchen door, dragging out a very badly injured Frankie.

"Take her in," the man who asked the questions said.

"Where are you taking me?" I fired at them. Nobody answered. I was being dragged out of the room; kicking and flailing did nothing to slow them down.

It was then that I realized they were all wearing the same uniform, and the logo said, 'North County Psychiatric Facility'.

"I'm not crazy!" I shouted, even though I knew that everyone, crazy or not, tried that line.

"I need the needle," the guy holding me shouted over my screams.

"No!" I hollered.

Nobody listened to me.

A needle was jammed into my shoulder.

The last thing I could remember was Ally crying, Tanner reassuring her that it would all be okay, and Frankie laying on the floor at their feet, bloodied and reaching out to me, completely unnoticed by any of the men taking me away.

EPILOGUE

My head was throbbing, my stomach was empty, and my muscles ached.

To my count, I had been laying in that hospital bed, drugged, and abandoned for the last three days.

It could very well have been more than that, but I had no way of knowing. There was no window in my room, no clock on my wall, and food was delivered at random times, when it was even delivered at all.

They had to chain my hands and legs to the bed the first day they brought me in, claiming that I was a fighter.

I did not have a fighting bone in my body. I just wanted to go home.

They were regular with the drugs, though.

It seemed every hour they were here with a full needle.

I hated the drowsy, sluggish feeling when they injected my body with whatever awful thing was in those needles.

It left me feeling weak, not in control of my own limbs.

"Visitor," rang the nurse's voice in my doorway.

Ally walked into the room and closed the door softly behind her, giving me a pitiful look.

"Aww, hunny." She rested a hand lightly on my arm. "How are you feeling?"

"Why are you doing this to me?" I hated the smug, fake look of sorrow she was gave me. I hated the gentle touch that I knew was staged. I hated the false love in her eyes. I hated her.

Her façade dropped, and she looked every bit as evil as I had realized she was.

"We need you out of the picture so we can do what we need to do."

"Why here?" I asked her. I wanted to cry, but I held onto my tough bravado.

"We need their drugs in your system." She shrugged like it was no big deal. "You see, you gave us the missing piece of the puzzle. We needed to figure out how to change you back into the queen. We can overdose you, easily. I actually just finished hacking their system to reschedule your next time. By my calculations, they'll be in here within the next—" She took a fake look at her watch that was not even on her wrist "—five minutes to give you an extra dose. It'll be enough to completely flatline you. You either die, and we win, or you become the queen, and the fun can really begin."

"Who are you?"

"Oh, I really am Sharie, I really am your most trusted advisor."

"Then why are you doing this to me? Why are you working for Tanner?"

"With Tanner," she corrected me. "I'm tired of being on the sidelines while you get all the glory and credit for my ideas. I'm taking over your kingdom, my Queen. And then I am going to merge with Tanner, and together we will be the most powerful fairies to have ever ruled."

So, Tanner was the king. I should have guessed that by now.

Ryker was right in warning me to stay away from him.

Ryker. Where was he? He could feel my emotions. He could sense where I was. Why had he not come to my rescue? Was he in on it, too?

Before I could ask anything else, a nurse came in, carrying a tray that I was quickly learning to dread.

"Time for your medicine!" she said way too cheerily. "Visiting time is over, sweetheart," she said to Ally.

"I was just leaving." She smiled her award-winning smile, waved a sad goodbye to me and left without another word.

"I really don't need it," I protested to the nurse. "I'm all better, I promise."

"Of course, dear," she said. She probably heard those things all the time.

If I had access to my arms or legs, I would have put up a fight. But seeing as how I had maximum restraints, I was forced to lay there and take the burning needle in my arm and wait for my heart to flatline.

It did not take long before my eyes grew heavy, my heart started to slow, and I struggled to breathe.

A second before I welcomed death, flashes of bright colors, new sights and sounds, people with different voices and looks flew behind my closed lids.

I remembered every detail from the moment I had been born, from the battles I fought and won, to the many secret moments I had shared with Ryker.

My memories had been returned to me, just in time for me to take in my very last breath.